DOWNFALL

A COMEDY SCI-FI ADVENTURE SERIES

BY

SAMLUCAS

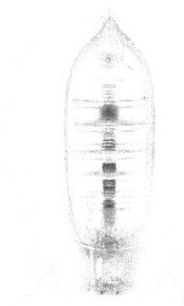

*...I've got some hemlock at the bottom
of the garden and I didn't want to get
the wrong plant and kill us all...*

BOOK THREE - PART ONE

© TITLE FONT & ILLUSTRATION BY SAM LUCAS
OSCAR PISCINE BOOK PUBLISHING

ISBN 978-1-7398855-3-3

Paperback Version

DOWNFALL PART ONE BY SAM LUCAS © 2022

WWW.SAMLUCASBOOKS.COM
e-mail:samlucasbooks@btinternet.com

PUBLISHER - OSCAR PISCINE BOOKS

Just over five light years away from Earth hidden in the foreboding darkness of space, a small unknown planet by the name of EgÁs lies behind the shadow of three milky, misty moons and two resolute, sedulous suns. Travelling north by north-east of the Alpha Centauri system, the planet can be first seen when the three moons of EgÁs move into the final phase of the winter solstice. On arrival, the traveller sees a lavish, bright lemon yellow sky that encompasses a golden globe abundant with life. In the lowlands, rich, lavish, colourful flowers decorate the landscape with an impressionistic splash of paint, whilst the highlands singular orange tone blends into the sky and the nothingness beyond. In the desert, golden sands drift into burnt ochre rock formations covering the past and long forgotten civilisations. In the forbidden territories, lie the highest peaks where big craggy mountain ranges acquiesce to luminous pools of hypnotic raspberry pink water. To the virgin traveller, the pools look like magnificent pockets of candyfloss that polka dot the effervescent surface as its shimmering veneer dances like jewels on a Victorian Christmas tree. In the distance, a grey, metallic empire rises out of the vivid, cloudless landscape, striking the planet with the dullness of a black and white crossword puzzle only to burst into a blinding corn yellow light to uncover the magnificent metropolis of MomÁdrac.

Beneath the surface, lain dormant for these past five thousand years, lie The Great Council of Arkanazak. In a sealed cavern beneath the ruined city of EgÁrob and the hot desert sands, King KÁnTdiE, leader and supreme ruler of the immortals, sits on his golden throne endlessly decaying amongst the 12 governing delegates of the Nog-Árrat MylÁ system. Each delegate, also in various states of decay, sit silently waiting on dusty marble chairs. The once grand gallery, where the control room of the universe buzzed with the noise of life, flashing consoles and colourful vibrant screens, now lies peaceful, silent and dead; a stillness found only in the eyes of a shark.

To the new inhabitants above, The Great Council of Arkanazak are just myth, a fanciful legend noted down through the years by ancient cave art and faded papyrus scrolls. To some unconventional thinkers, historians and archaeologists, the Council represent the ultimate answer to planet EgÁs's birth. The validation of the Council's existence will unveil the truth to a society lost in the fog of unilateral thinking and bourgeois materialism.

The Council now wait, as they have waited all these long years - dead, but not dead; outsmarted by their own creation and cursed to an endless sea of time and nihility. In their protected vault they sit and wait and wait and wait. Outside, day turns to night and back to day again, war becomes peace, peace becomes war, over and over again. In the end, time will be their salvation, time will eventually set them free. Until then, they continue to decompose into small powdery piles of dust. Only the return of the golden Medallion of Life can set them free, but that has been lost for millennia and wait they must; but beneath the dust and the corrosion of time, a glimmer of hope flashes in the darkness, a solitary button pulses red.

ACT I. SCENE I

Our scene starts in the ruined reception area of the Four Seasons hotel in Moscow. It is Thursday evening 7.45pm, 16th October 2025. The alien shuttle has now returned to its sealed ovoid shape and looks like a large lump of coal nestled in ash and cinders on top of a scorched, burnt carpet. The main entrance to the reception area is missing and the view to the outside street shows a trail of destruction. Small fires burn within the newly made runway and car alarms ringout in the street. A company of girl scouts lay huddled in a group behind a white minibus and look on at the carnage. In the distance the sound of trucks approaching can be heard. Inside the hotel, the Russian Prime Minister is standing next to a waiter and looks on bewildered at Dmitry and Yuri and quickly becomes flummoxed by the insane number of questions the Press are asking. Dmitry and Yuri look very happy and hug each other. From behind the reception area, a small buxom woman wearing a pink trouser suit emerges from the debris and stands up. Yuri takes out his little tartan friend, retrieves a cigarette and lights it, takes a deep draw and lets out a satisfying cloud of smoke.

> *(The Prime Minister begins to address the members of the Press, then stops.)*

P.M. KANTCOUGHSKY
You must excuse me, I seemed to have dropped my fish...

> *(The Prime Minister turns to the waiter next to him.)*

...Could I get another fish please, this one is spoiled.

> *(The waiter nods and walks off.)*

PRESS REPORTER
Prime Minister, how can you explain the miraculous appearance of Dmitry Usakov and Yuri Chekov at your banquet tonight when they are supposed to be dead?

P.M. KANTCOUGHSKY
Is that who it is? Forgive me, I couldn't see without my glasses. You will have to excuse me, I have dropped my fish - this is a disaster, I have halibut in my shoe.

                    RECEPTIONIST
Excuse me, sir?

        (The receptionist points her
        finger at Yuri.)

                      YURI
Who me?

                    RECEPTIONIST
Yes, you. You can't smoke that
cigarette in here, it's against the
rules.

        (Yuri looks around at the big
        hole where the hotel doors
        used to be, then back at the
        receptionist.)

                      YURI
You can't be serious? Are you seeing
what I am seeing?

                    RECEPTIONIST
Yes I am, but carpet cigarette burns
cost the hotel industry millions of
Rubles before the smoking ban. Put
that cigarette out or kindly leave.

                     DMITRY
C'mon Yuri, let's get some air before
Press pounce on us or big report is
made for smoking in public place
without licence.

(The Prime Minister retreats behind the banquet doors and the Press run towards Yuri and Dmitry.)

YURI

Some air, yes. That would be nice; to breathe clean air with the evening sun on our faces. The world is a beautiful place Dmitry, I don't think I will take it for granted ever again.

(Dmitry and Yuri walk outside the hotel and down the steps. Behind them, members of the Press race towards them at breakneck speed. Yuri throws his cigarette to the ground.)

YURI

Here they come!

(As Yuri's cigarette falls to the ground, a deafening blast comes from the inside of the hotel. Glass, bricks, metal and furniture fly through the air. A furnace blast rushes through the hotel reception and the members of the Press burst into flames as a fireball engulfs the area. Another explosion occurs and the building starts to

*collapse. Yuri and Dmitry
are knocked to the floor and
lie on the road outside the
hotel.)*

DMITRY
Are you alright Yuri?

*(Yuri rolls onto his side and
gets to his feet and dusts
himself off.)*

YURI
Yes, I think so. I have all my
limbs, but my ears hurt.

*(Yuri helps Dmitry up and
they look at the ruined hotel
behind them.)*

DMITRY
What the hell happened?...

*(Smoke billows up from the
rubble and intense fires rage
from the building's
foundations. Electric wires
spark on the ground, earthing
wildly in small puddles of
grey water. Screams for help
cry out and a blanket of
thick dust covers everything
and everyone.)*

...Do you think your wife was inside?

                    YURI
I don't know, but I think Ivanka
would have made an excuse not to go
to banquet; a broken fingernail or
grey hair that needed dying. If she
was inside, she would have only been
laughing about our situation and
groping that scumbag Anatoly. If she
is dead, I will put flowers on her
grave and mourn her loss. If she is
alive, I will cut off her allowance.
You know what Newton said?

        *(Dmitry catches his breath
        and sits down on a lone car
        wheel amongst the debris and
        starts to remove his space
        suit to reveal a very dusty
        grey boiler suit underneath.)*

                    DMITRY
Yes, something about every action has
a reaction.

                    YURI
Did he say that, I did not realise
you knew Newton?

        (Yuri rubs his right elbow.)

                    DMITRY
Everybody knows the great scientist

Isaac Newton, well anybody who went to school.

                    YURI
I think we have our Newton's mixed up, the Newton I knew lived next door to parents' house when I was boy, this fellow you know is stranger to me and first time I am hearing about him. My Newton's first name was Albert.

          (Dmitry looks up at Yuri.)

                    DMITRY
That figures. I am almost afraid to ask, but what did your neighbour Albert Newton say?

                    YURI
What was it again, ah yes. *'If you like to eat eggs, don't buy a cockerel, If you buy a cockerel, you will have no eggs to eat.'* ...It was something like that. And then something else about fields of corn and a bucket of water. He was a wise man for a bus conductor...

          *(Yuri picks up a coin from
          the street and puts it in his
          space suit top pocket.)*

...What about your wife? We should

go and look for her?

                    DMITRY
Don't worry. She won't be inside.

                    YURI
How do you know?

                    DMITRY
We have been separated for the past
year, and we haven't lived together
for the last three months. That's
why we did not see or hear about her
when we were believed to be dead.

                    YURI
I am sorry Dmitry, you should have
told me.

                    DMITRY
It was my fault, I am a drunk. I
drove her away. I have only just
realised it, but it's the truth.

        (Across the street amongst
        the wreckage, a company of
        Girl Scouts aged between 5
        and 7, huddle around a white
        minibus. One of the girls is
        crying and she is holding a
        headless teddy bear. Dmitry
        and Yuri notice the group of
        girls and go over to comfort
        them. In the distance the

*sound of sirens can be heard
- police cars, fire engines
and ambulances race towards
the scene. A low rumble from
heavy trucks can also be
heard and felt as the city
vibrates under their weight
and presence.)*

                    YURI
Don't worry everything will be
alright...

          *(Yuri gets down on his knees
          to be at the same height as
          the girls.)*

...The emergency services are on the
way. Is anybody hurt.

                    GIRL SCOUT 1
No, but we can't find our leader Miss
Decapinovsky.

                    YURI
I am sure she is around here
somewhere...

          *(Yuri looks around to face
          Dmitry.)*

...Dmitry? Go look for their scout
leader.

                    DMITRY
Okay, I will see if I can find her.

                   GIRL SCOUT 2
Benjamin has lost his head.

     *(The girl holds up a scruffy
     looking teddy bear with no
     head.)*

                     YURI
I think your teddy bear has seen
better days, but do not cry...

     *(Yuri reaches inside his suit
     and pulls out his trusty
     tartan trousered friend. He
     removes his cigarettes from
     the stomach pouch and shows
     it to the little girl.)*

...Look at what I have here. He is a
very special bear. So very special.
He is only one of his kind, he is
first cosmonaut bear in history, the
very first bear to travel into outer
space. I have had this bear for over
40 years, so I would not part with
him lightly, it would have to be a
very special person to own such a
bear...

     *(The little girl scout looks
     on in wonder and stops
     crying. She starts to hold*

the yellow tartan leg of
Yuri's bear and drops her
decapitated ball of fluff.)

...You look like a very special
person. If you promise to look after
him, I will give him to you - his
name is Rupertvich.

> GIRL SCOUT 2

I promise.

(Yuri hands over the bear and
the girl smiles and cuddles
her new friend. Dmitry comes
from around the back of the
minibus holding the Scout
leader, Miss Decapinovsky.
She has a bump on her head
and a cut on her leg and is
limping.)

> YURI

You are wounded?

> MISS DECAPINOVSKY

It is nothing, I am alright. Thank
you for looking after the children, I
must have fainted. Do you know what
happened?

> YURI

The hotel was destroyed, there must
have been a bomb of some kind.

(Dmitry lets go of Miss Decapinovsky and places her on the ground by the children. She counts the children, pats their heads, smiles and turns to face Yuri and Dmitry.)

MISS DECAPINOVSKY
It is probably that terrorist group O.F.E, they've been pamphlet bombing all of the big food venues in the city for the last two days. They've also let off stink bombs, thrown flour parcels and rotten eggs; and resorted to the odd fart cushion on public transportation, but I guess they must have upped their game.

DMITRY
I haven't heard anything about them for awhile?

MISS DECAPINOVSKY
What? Have you been living under a rock the last 48 hours, the *Organisation for Food Equality* have been on a spree, the news has been everywhere.

DMITRY
Forgive me, but Yuri and I have been out of town without a T.V. or

newspaper the last few days.

    (Miss Decapinovsky starts to
    stare at Yuri quizzically.)

         MISS DECAPINOVSKY
Yuri? You're... You're Yuri Chekov,
the cosmonaut that died on the *Space
Station*...

    (The woman turns white and
    looks concerned and anxious.
    She turns to look at Dmitry.)

...And you're that other fellow,
Dmitry Usakov.

    (The woman gets to her feet.)

...That must mean ...That must mean
...I am dead. I'm only 27, I had my
whole life ahead of me. I had
tickets to see La Bohème at the
Bolshoi theatre tomorrow night and I
had just passed my advanced driving
test...

    (The woman gets to her feet
    and starts to talk to
    herself.)

...This can't be happening. What a
time to die, who's going to take my
Zharkoye stew out of the oven in 3
hours time, it'll be ruined.

                    YURI
You're not dead. We are alive. We
didn't die on *Space Station*, we made
it home didn't we Dmitry?

                    DMITRY
That's right. We made it back.

     (Yuri gets up from his
     crouched position and starts
     to dance around.)

                    YURI
Ooo, ouch, ooo, ooo. Something is
very hot!

     (A small hole can be seen in
     the back leg of Yuri's Space
     suit and smoke is emanating
     from the hole.)

                    DMITRY
You are on fire Yuri. Quickly, take
off your suit...

     (Yuri takes off his space
     suit and throws it on the
     floor and rolls around in the
     dirt.)

...It's okay, you can stop now, the
fire is out.

     (Dmitry helps Yuri up from

the ground.)

YURI

Thank you...

> *(Yuri brushes himself off and grabs his space suit. He takes out the laser gun and waves it towards Dmitry, Miss Decapinovsky and the group of girl scouts.)*

...I better not leave this behind, you never know when it will come in handy, and I don't want some young hoodlum finding it and causing havoc.

DMITRY

Stop waving that thing about and put it somewhere safe, you are frightening the girls.

> *(Police cars, fire engines and ambulances arrive on the street. Behind them are two big army trucks, military motorbikes and jeeps. A platoon of soldiers jump out of the trucks and surround the area outside the hotel. AK-47 rifles, sniper rifles, hand guns and a sonic weapon (LRAD) are now being held at Yuri, Dmitry, Miss*

*Decapinovsky and the band of
girl scouts. The police and
the other emergency services
wait for the army to move in
first.)*

SOLDIER 1

You two men? Slowly put your hands
in the air and move away from the
children and the lady on your right.
You on the left, put the gun down.
Make any sudden movements or attempt
to escape and we will shoot.

*(Yuri puts the laser gun down
on the ground and moves away.
Dmitry follows close behind
him. The girl scouts and
miss Decapinovsky don't move
a muscle and stay huddled
close to the minibus. The
soldiers move in and rush
towards Dmitry and Yuri
shouting out various orders.)*

SOLDIER 2

Get on your knees. Put your hands
behind your head.

*(Dmitry and Yuri do as
instructed and are
handcuffed. They are pulled
back on their feet and
dragged quickly towards the
back of an army truck.)*

                    DMITRY
What are you doing? Why have you
handcuffed us? Where are you taking
us?

                   SOLDIER 3
To military prison. Where did you
think you were going?

                    DMITRY
I thought you might be taking us
somewhere safe away from here.

                   SOLDIER 3
Butrayka prison is very safe, it is
where we put all political
terrorists. It is our most secure
prison in Russia. You will be very
safe.

        *(Yuri is slightly behind
        Dmitry and can only hear the
        odd word Dmitry and the
        soldier are saying.)*

                     YURI
What is happening?

                    DMITRY
Don't worry, I am handling it...

        *(Dmitry addresses the soldier
        again as the sergeant of the
        platoon walks over.)*

...What political terrorists? We are Russian cosmonauts Yuri Chekov and Dmitry Usakov!

(The soldier stops walking and looks at the sergeant. The sergeant has heard what Dmitry is saying and puts him into the back of the truck.)

SERGEANT

Yuri Chekov and Dmitry Usakov you say? I think you might have come up with a better story than that. Those two are dead, they were being honoured with a remembrance banquet in the very hotel you just blew up. Cut the nonsense Viktor, the games up, you and your friend Alexander over there are well known terrorists in Russia...

(The sergeant places Dmitry on a bench seat and checks his handcuffs. The sergeant's accent and locution are peculiar for a Russian native and have British influences. Sergeant Smithsky is 6ft 5 inches tall and is well built.)

...What else would you be doing outside a bombed out hotel?...

(The sergeant takes a seat opposite Dmitry.)

...And I suppose that gun your friend was waving about at those girl scouts was just some innocent fun?

(The sergeant leans forward towards Dmitry.)

...Terrorising 5 year old girls is even low for you Victor. With a rap sheet like yours; Well, you're for it this time. Once the prison officers give you a good going over, you'll be escorted straight to the gallows. It's the hangman this time...

(The sergeant sits back and smiles.)

...There's no escaping it.

DMITRY
We were not threatening anyone, my partner was merely retrieving his gun from his space suit. I don't even know who this Viktor you speak of is. There is something wrong here, I want to speak to someone in charge?

SGT. SMITHSKY
Don't you worry, you'll get a chance to speak to someone alright. Now,

sit there and be quiet.

(Yuri enters the truck and sits next to Dmitry.)

                    YURI
How is it going Dmitry, did you
manage to work everything out?

                    DMITRY
Not quite, but I think we might need
a good lawyer and our passports.

                    YURI
Why, are we going on a trip? I hope
it is somewhere warm.

Scene fades.

ACT I. SCENE 2

A small convoy of military vehicles move south out of Moscow, two *Zil-131* general purpose trucks, a Dnepr *K750M* motorcycle with side car and two *UAZ-469* jeeps. Inside the back of the first truck in the convoy, Yuri and Dmitry sit on a bench seat along with 8 soldiers: a sergeant, a corporal and 6 privates. Yuri has been asleep since he got into the truck and lies slumped over on Dmitry's shoulder. Outside, the light is fading as the evening wears on and the smell of rain is in the air. It has been 27 minutes since they first got into the truck and they are now in rural russia heading towards the Oka river.

> *(A bump in the road moves Yuri from his seat and he wakes up, wipes his eyes, tries to fold his arms, then yawns.)*

                    YURI
I don't know about you Dmitry, but I am ready for a light supper, a bath, then bed. Perhaps a lightly smoked kipper with some chicory tossed in a walnut and sesame dressing, followed by a raspberry sorbet.

(Dmitry looks out of the back of the truck at Moscow in the distance. He turns to face Yuri.)

DMITRY

That's sounds like a good idea, perhaps if you ask the sergeant over there if he knows any good hotels that could possibly accommodate us at short notice.

(Yuri looks over at the sergeant.)

YURI

Excuse me? My friend and I were wondering if you knew of any hotels in the area?

SGT. SMITHSKY

Funny aren't you, but don't worry, we always make sure you get a wash, a meal and a bed.

(Yuri nudges Dmitry's arm.)

YURI

Did you hear that Dmitry, they are going to give us a bed for the night and some food. I hope they have feather pillows, I left mine on the *Space Station*.

DMITRY
What are you talking about, feather
pillows? We will be lucky to get an
old iron bed with a scratchy woollen
blanket. But I can assure you one
thing, you will not have any trouble
sleeping after they have hit you in
the face a few times and thrown icy
cold buckets of water over you for
five hours.

(Yuri looks puzzled.)

YURI
I think I have missed something here.
Where are we going Dmitry?

*(Dmitry looks at Yuri with
exasperation.)*

DMITRY
They are taking us to Butrayka
prison, didn't you notice you were
wearing handcuffs?

YURI
Prison! Why, what have we done? We
are heroes.

*(Dmitry looks over to the
sergeant.)*

DMITRY
Excuse me sergeant, but I don't

suppose you have any proof or record of the crimes my friend and I have been charged with?

(The sergeant reaches inside his pocket and takes out a criminal record pertaining to Viktor Popov and Alexander Ivanov. He hands it over to Dmitry. Dmitry then hands it over to Yuri to look at.)

YURI

What is this...

(Yuri reads the paper.)

...They can't be serious Dmitry, everybody knows who we are, our pictures have been published in hundreds of newspapers and magazines...

(Yuri reads on.)

...Wanted for acts of treason, terrorism, murder, kidnapping, arson, drug trafficking and distribution, larceny and conspiracy to commit fraud...

(Yuri turns the Criminal Record over to see if there is anything on the other side.)

...Who is this Viktor Popov and Alexander Ivanov? They seem like real troublemakers.

                    DMITRY
For the time being Yuri, it is you and I.

        (Yuri addresses the
        sergeant.)

                    YURI
This is ridiculous, we are Yuri Chekov and Dmitry Usakov; the famous Russian cosmonauts that have freed our world from the enslavement of the Dome and destroyers of the alien monster ship.

        (Dmitry grabs Yuri's arm.)

                    DMITRY
Yuri? They know nothing about Dome or ship, nobody on Earth does, it is a secret - remember?

                    YURI
Oh, that is right. Then what are we going to do? What is going to happen to us?

                    SGT. SMITHSKY
Be quiet! Enough of this stupid

chit-chat. The next one of you to speak will get a fat lip.

    (Dmitry and Yuri retreat back into their seats and look down at the floor. The corporal leans forward to catch the gaze of the sergeant.)

          CORPORAL MILLEROVSKY
Y'know *Sarg*, they do bear a striking resemblance to Yuri Chekov and Dmitry Usakov...

    (The corporal is a small wiry looking chap with a thick black moustache. His accent is also peculiar to this region of Russia. He looks at Dmitry and Yuri and then back at the sergeant.)

...And our orders were a bit unusual, even bordering fallacious. It's not common practice to take criminals directly to a military prison when they are not military personnel. They haven't even been formerly charged with anything. Perhaps something is a bit erroneous with all this. We should contact General Spuriovsky at head quarters to verify our orders.

                    SGT. SMITHSKY
Erroneous? Fallacious? You're not
one of those educated troublemakers I
hope? There is nothing worse than a
good Samaritan in the army, they
always get the whole platoon wiped
out. It's one of the biggest jinxes
you can have. Believe you me, you
start questioning the powers that be
and you will soon be in hot water.
You better address your attitude my
lad and keep your opinions to
yourself. Who cares who these two
are, that's not our business. Orders
are orders, arrest anyone on site -
that's straight from the top.
Nobody's going to be disturbing
General Spuriovsky at 8.30pm on a
Thursday evening. Thursday evening
is *Bridge* night, contacting the
General on *Bridge* night is
justification for dismissal and
possible grounds for a court marshal.
Now sit back and be quiet, we will be
at Butrayka in the next hour; we will
sort it out then.

    (Outside, the night is
    falling and the sky is
    growing darker. The lights of
    Moscow and surrounding
    townships can been seen
    through the back window of
    the truck. Dmitry whispers
    to Yuri.)

                    DMITRY
I hope you still have some whisky on
you Yuri, my throat is parched?

                    YURI
I hate to be bearer of bad news, but
no. My whisky is inside space suit
pocket lying in street in Moscow, but
at least I have my cigarettes.

          *(Through the back window of
          the truck, Dmitry can see
          what looks like a shower of
          meteorites and shooting stars
          falling over Moscow.)*

                    DMITRY
Yuri?

          (Yuri looks at Dmitry.)

                    YURI
Yes, what is it?

                    DMITRY
Look out the window.

          *(Yuri opens his eyes and
          looks out the back window.
          More meteorites and long
          glowing strands of bright
          white and orange are starting
          to hit the city of Moscow. A
          few small explosions can be*

seen.)

                    YURI
We are under attack. Who would do
such a thing. Quick, call the army.

        *(A cluster of meteorites
        start to fall down on Moscow
        and the surrounding area,
        moving closer to Dmitry and
        Yuri. The sound of
        explosions and high speed
        projectiles can now be
        heard.)*

                    DMITRY
Calm down Yuri, I think I know what
it is.

        *(The sergeant and his men
        look on at the show of
        fireworks and mayhem.)*

                    YURI
What is it?

                    DMITRY
It is alien spaceship breaking up in
atmosphere.

                    YURI
Then this is our fault, we did this.

        (Just behind them large

*fragments of spaceship start
to explode on the road.)*

YURI
Dmitry, they're getting closer.

*(All around the military
convoy, large chunks of metal
fall and explode on the
ground.)*

SGT. SMITHSKY
Corporal Millerovsky, get your men on
the ready.

CPL. MILLEROVSKY
Aye, Aye *Sarg.*

*(Behind them, the truck
carrying the second platoon
are hit by a large falling
object and it explodes into a
ball of fire. All around the
convoy huge chunks of red hot
metal impact the earth. One
of the UAZ-469 jeeps is hit
and it is thrown in the air.
The second jeep swerves off
the road and crashes in a
ditch.)*

SGT. SMITHSKY
Private Driverov, put your foot on
the gas and get us the hell out of

here?

                    PVT. DRIVEROV
Yes, *Sarg*.

>   *(The truck begins to pick up
>   speed, but is suddenly hit by
>   a large piece of debris on
>   the bonnet and catches fire.
>   The driver, 4 other privates
>   and the corporal are hit by
>   shrapnel and are killed
>   instantly. The truck rolls
>   down an embankment and Yuri
>   and Dmitry are thrown from
>   the truck along with the
>   sergeant. Inside the truck,
>   the remaining privates try to
>   jump out as it goes off a
>   cliff; they disappear over
>   the edge.*

Scene fades.

ACT 1. SCENE 3

Small fires burn throughout the immediate landscape and bigger forest fires can be seen in the distance. Yuri, Dmitry and the sergeant lay dispersed in the bushes and undergrowth of the embankment. The fire storm has moved on and can be heard up ahead in the distance. It is now night-time and is quite dark amongst the debris field of fires.

                    DMITRY
Yuri, where are you? I can't see anything, I am stuck in a gorse bush.

     *(Yuri is lying in a ditch
     and his legs are soaked with
     water. He starts to move.)*

                    YURI
Hold on, I am in ditch. Where are you? Shout out?

                    DMITRY
Here, I'm over here.

     (Dmitry rustles the bush.)

                    YURI
I see you, hold on.

*(Yuri finds Dmitry and pulls
him out of the bush.)*

DMITRY
Thank you Yuri, there is nothing
worse than a gorse bush...

*(Dmitry brushes himself
down.)*

...That is better. Horrible scratchy
thing, there should be a law against
shrubbery. Imagine making a
beautiful yellow flower that smells
of coconut, and then filling rest of
plant with spikes and *jabby* barbs.
It is a sadistic pointless annoyance
that should be burnt...

*(Dmitry pulls some spikes and
spines out of his arms and
trouser leg.)*

...Stupid weed. At least in space we
did not have problem of plant life.
C'mon, we've got to get out of here
and get these handcuffs off. See if
you can find anyone with a key...

*(A noise is heard on the
embankment, south of their
position.)*

...What's that? Who's there?

*(A moaning noise is heard
again.)*

SGT. SMITHSKY
Sgt. Smithsky, I...

*(The sergeant gets a sharp
stab of pain.)*

...I am here. I'm hurt.

YURI
What should we do?

DMITRY
He might have a key, let's go and
see...

*(Dmitry brushes himself down
one more time.)*

...Don't worry, we are coming.

*(Dmitry and Yuri make their
way to the sergeant's
position on the embankment.
The sergeant has a large
metal rod through his chest
pinning him to the ground.)*

SGT. SMITHSKY
How does it look?

DMITRY
Not good. The rod has punctured your
left lung and you are losing a lot of
blood. You have multiple shrapnel
wounds and your right foot is
missing.

YURI
Dmitry, could you not have a better
bedside manner?

SGT. SMITHSKY
That's alright, he speaks the truth.
I'm done for. I knew it was all over
as soon as I heard Cpl. Millerovsky
utter the word 'fallacious'. There
is no place for that type of lexicon
in the army, two syllables is usually
our limit. You know what they say...

> (The sergeant moans for a few
> seconds and finds it
> difficult to breathe.)

...Never trust a man with a thick
moustache and a circuitous tongue.

> (The sergeant takes a final
> breath and utters his last
> words.)

SGT. SMITHSKY
Remember these words, *'Honest Frank
is forthcoming and candid'*...

                    DMITRY
He's dead.

                    YURI
Honest Frank is forthcoming and
candid? What does that mean, and why
would I want to remember it?

                    DMITRY
Who knows? He was dying...

        (Dmitry looks around then
        searches the sergeant for the
        key to their handcuffs. He
        finds it in a top pocket and
        releases Yuri and then
        himself from their shackles.)

                    DMITRY
...C'mon, let's get out of here
before reinforcements arrive. Get to
the road.

        (Dmitry and Yuri scramble up
        the embankment and get onto
        the road. Small fires burn
        and there are huge chunks of
        metal everywhere.)

                    YURI
What a mess! This is our fault. If
we hadn't blown up that ship, this
wouldn't of happened...

*(Dmitry and Yuri walk amongst
the fires and debris. Small
fires, big metal shards and
fallen burnt trees stretch
off into the distance.)*

...What are we going to do now
Dmitry?

DMITRY
We are going to get out of here,
that's what we are going to do...

*(As they walk along the road,
they come across the Dnepr
K750M motorcycle with side
car that was part of the
convoy. The driver is dead,
but the motorcycle is
untouched and lies in a
ditch.)*

...Look, it's a motorcycle!

*(Dmitry runs over to the
motorcycle.)*

...Help me get this guy off of this
thing, so we can drag it on road.

*(Yuri walks over to the
motorcycle.)*

YURI
Is he dead?

                    DMITRY
Yes.

                     YURI
How do you know?

                    DMITRY
He has a big hole where his heart
should be. That is usually a good
indication someone is dead. Now help
me push him off this thing...

     *(Dmitry and Yuri pull the man
     from the motorcycle and drag
     it onto the road.)*

...Hurry up and get in sidecar, we
don't have much time...

     *(The sound of vehicles can be
     heard approaching their
     position. Dmitry tries to
     start the motorcycle.)*

...Listen! Trucks!

     *(Dmitry pushes his foot down
     on the kick start but the
     motorcycle just gurgles and
     splutters. From behind them,
     they can see military
     vehicles and fire trucks
     moving closer to their
     position.)*

                    DMITRY
Piece of junk. C'mon start. I never
did like motorcycles, they are just
petrol strimmers with wheels. Stupid
contraption, it has probably spent
more time in workshop than on road -
Russian crap; just start!

        *(From behind them a fire
        engine, a UAZ-469 jeep and a
        Zil-131 general purpose truck
        hurtle into sight. Machine
        gun fire rains down on Yuri
        and Dmitry.)*

                    YURI
Dmitry, get us out of here, they are
shooting at us!

        *(Dmitry kicks the pedal
        again, and the motorcycle
        starts. Dmitry lets the
        throttle rip and they speed
        off down the road.)*

                    DMITRY
Keep your head down.

        *(Fire, Debris and fallen
        branches cover the road and
        Dmitry steers through the
        carnage at high speed.
        Behind Yuri and Dmitry a
        convoy of military vehicles
        has now appeared, led by a*

UAZ-469 *jeep. The bigger vehicles in the convoy are struggling to maintain Dmitry's pace, but the UAZ-469 jeep is on their tail. A soldier shoots an AK-47 rifle from the passenger seat of the jeep.)*

                    YURI
Dmitry, they are gaining, do
something!

                    DMITRY
What would you like me to do. We are
too heavy. That sidecar is causing a
lot of drag, see if you can uncouple
it.

                    YURI
Why would I do that?

                    DMITRY
So we don't have as much weight.

                    YURI
What will happen to me?

                    DMITRY
You can jump on the back behind me.
Yuri turn your brain on, and do
something.

(Shots ring out past Yuri's head as they swerve violently down the road. Debris and fires are still scattered about the place and hinder Dmitry's driving and speed. The jeep is gaining on them, but also smacks into debris on the road.)

                    YURI
I have found instruction booklet for
sidecar...

(Yuri scans through the booklet and reads aloud.)

...Index. Uncoupling of sidecar page
4...

(A large tree that is on fire begins to fall on the road. Dmitry, Yuri and the pursuing jeep get past before the road is blocked. The other military vehicles can no longer follow. The rat-a-tat-tat of an AK-47 rifle continues to fire rounds at high speed in Dmitry and Yuri's direction.)

...Remove fixing mounting bolt
(Fig.A) at front with supplied 13mm
spanner and repeat process for rear

mounting bolt (Fig.B)...

*(Yuri looks around for the
13mm spanner and finds it in
a small bag attached to the
inside wall of the side car.
He begins to remove the bolt
from the rear of the bike.)*

...I am going to remove the sidecar.

                    DMITRY
Okay.

*(Dmitry sees a roadblock up
ahead in the distance, and
slows down a little. The
jeep start to gain on them.)*

                    YURI
That is one bolt...

*(Yuri holds the bolt in the
air, smiles and then throws
it.)*

...Why are we slowing down?

                    DMITRY
There is a roadblock up ahead.

*(The sidecar starts to wobble
violently and breaks free.)*

                    YURI
Oh, no!

                   DMITRY
Jump Yuri!

        (*Yuri jumps from the sidecar
        onto the back of the
        motorcycle. The sidecar hits
        a branch in the road and
        flips upside down and flies
        towards the following jeep,
        landing on its bonnet. The
        Jeep careers off the road and
        down a bank ending up in a
        lake.*)

                    YURI
We did it Dmitry, we escaped.

                   DMITRY
I don't think we are in the clear
yet...

        (*Up ahead the roadblock is
        getting closer. Dmitry spies
        an old farm track on his
        right and turns down it. The
        fuel gauge on the motorcycle
        is nearly on empty and the
        motorcycle is beginning to
        splutter and cough.*)

...We are nearly out of gas, the tank

has a hole in it. Keep an eye out
for a building so we can stash this
thing.

                    YURI
Okay, I will look...

          (Yuri tries to see in the
          darkness and spots a
          farmhouse on the left.)

...Turn left up here, I see a house.

          (Dmitry turns left up the
          track and heads towards a
          farmhouse. The house is
          boarded up and it looks like
          nobody's home. To the right
          of the house are outbuildings
          and various small sheds. The
          motorbike runs out of fuel
          and they drift the remaining
          40 feet to the house.)

                    DMITRY
Quickly, push the bike into shed.

          (Yuri and Dmitry dismount the
          motorbike and put it in a
          shed. They grab an old
          tarpaulin and cover it up.
          They place some old pallets
          around it and walk back
          outside. Down the hill,
          about 2 miles away, the

*roadblock is clearly visible.
Police cars, army trucks,
ambulances and a helicopter
block the road. A platoon of
30-40 men walk up and down
surveying the area
accompanied by 15-20
emergency service workers.*

YURI
That looks like a real hornet's nest
down there.

*(Yuri puts a cigarette in his
mouth and goes to light it.
Dmitry pulls it out of his
mouth and throws it on the
floor.)*

DMITRY
I would appreciate it if you didn't
smoke, I am covered in petrol.

YURI
Sorry, I needed a little comfort. My
mind is racing. What are we going to
do Dmitry?

*(Dmitry walks over to the
farmhouse and pulls some
boards down from the front
door.)*

                    DMITRY
We are going to see if there is water
in this house and a change of
clothes.

                    YURI
Do you think we should be breaking
into this house, it wasn't one of the
items on the list of our crimes.

                    DMITRY
Shut up for five minutes and give me
a hand with these boards.

        *(Dmitry and Yuri begin to
        pull the planks of wood away
        from the front door to reveal
        the handle. Far off into the
        distance a rumble and crack
        can be heard. Another boom,
        followed by an even bigger
        boom echoing across the
        hills, and then, a bright
        flash lights up the sky and a
        big red fireball 300 feet
        wide descends from the black
        sky.)*

                    YURI
What was that?

                    DMITRY
I don't know. Go take a look.

(Yuri walks around the corner of the outbuilding and sees a huge fireball in the sky.)

YURI
Dmitry, come quick!

(Dmitry drops a plank of wood on the floor and goes to see Yuri, then looks up at the fireball.)

DMITRY
Now what?

YURI
Dmitry what is happening?

DMITRY
I am not sure, but if I had to guess, I would say that is big part of alien ship coming in for crash landing.

(Dmitry and Yuri look on at the spectacle in awe as it descends from the clouds. The wind begins to pick up and small parcels of straw begin to blow about the farmyard.)

YURI
How far away would you say that is?

                    DMITRY
It is a good distance, about 15 to 20
miles away. Come, let's get inside.
When that thing hits the ground,
there is going to be trouble.

        *(Yuri and Dmitry pull the
        last planks of wood blocking
        the door and force their way
        in. The wind is getting
        stronger and the metal farm
        gates outside begin to rattle
        and groan. The weather vane
        on the farmhouse roof starts
        to spin.)*

                    DMITRY
Close the door.

        *(Dmitry and Yuri make their
        way inside the house and
        crawl under a pine table in
        the kitchen. Approximately
        22 miles away, a large chunk
        of metal hits the Earth and
        lands in a big lake near the
        town of Tulla. Huge
        mountains of water burst into
        the air causing a cloud of
        steam to race through the
        nearby forest like an eerie
        blanket of fog. The ground
        shakes and moans and a small
        earthquake rings out in all
        directions.)*

                    DMITRY
Keep your head down Yuri. Here it
comes.

          (The ground begins to shake
          and a cloud of dust rushes
          past the farmhouse. After a
          few minutes, the ground stops
          shaking and the wind falls to
          a light breeze.)

                    YURI
Is it over.

                    DMITRY
Yes, I think so.

Scene fades.

ACT I. SCENE 4

Inside the farmhouse, Yuri and Dmitry emerge from underneath the kitchen table and get to their feet. Yuri fumbles in the darkness to find a light switch and walks blindly around, touching everything from wall clocks to rolling pins. He finds it by the kitchen door frame and flicks it to the 'on' position - the power is still connected and the room fills with light. The kitchen is rustic and mostly made up of pine cupboards. They start to look through the cupboards for food and to their surprise, they are full of cans and jars: pickled cabbage, beetroot, fish, sour cream, peas, carrots, potatoes, custard and rice pudding and lots more. In the other compartments, they find tea, coffee, hot chocolate and tinned milk, cups, plates, cutlery and everything else associated with a well stocked kitchen. Dmitry turns on the taps at a butler sink and water comes out; he notices an emersion switch and turns it on.

                    DMITRY
Finally, we are getting a break. Twenty minutes and we will have hot water. I hope this place has a shower.

(Dmitry washes his hands at the sink and dries them on a dish towel.)

YURI

Hot water, what a luxury. I have to say Dmitry, you have looked better and a wash would improve your blackened face dramatically...

(Dmitry stares at Yuri.)

...But it is that reek of gasoline coming from your clothes that is the most offensive, it gives you a real authentic hobo quality...

(Dmitry replaces the dish towel and stares back at Yuri.)

...All you need now is a cane and you could pass for Charlie Chaplin.

DMITRY

You don't look so hot yourself. You are a man of two halves, your trousers are wet and stink of sewage and your top has more holes than a golf course...

(Dmitry starts to smile.)

...And your face, that is another story, it looks like the famous

French mime artist Marcel Marceau on
a bad day.

(They both laugh out loud.)

                    YURI
Dmitry, don't make me laugh, it hurts
too much. I have bruises on my
bruises and bumps on my bumps.

                  DMITRY
You will feel better when you get
under that shower and get some food
in your stomach.

                    YURI
Yes, I suppose I will, but do you
think we should be using electric and
stealing food from cupboards, what
about people who live here?

                  DMITRY
We will leave them an IOU, and send
them a cheque when we get out of this
mess. It must be somebody's holiday
home, that's why it is boarded up.
Under the circumstances, I am sure
they won't mind if we make ourselves
at home.

     (Dmitry picks up a kettle,
     adds water from the sink and
     switches it on. He takes two
     cups from the cupboard and

places them on the counter.)

YURI
So, you think we will get out of fix?
It would seem we have become the
famous fugitives Alexander Ivanov and
Viktor Popov wanted for crimes of
terrorism.

DMITRY
If we can get to a big newspaper like
the *Moscow Times* or a News station
before we get shot, then yes, I think
we have a chance to blow this thing
open and survive. We are too well
known as Russian cosmonauts, we just
have to stay alive long enough to
make it public knowledge...

(The kettle boils.)

...Coffee?

YURI
Yes, please.

DMITRY
I am afraid it is instant, will that
do?

YURI
At this moment in time, even idea of
hot water is making me tingle.

(Dmitry makes the coffee and they sit at the table.)

                    YURI
Aah, that's better, a real treat.

                    DMITRY
Yes, a real treat.

(They sit in silence for ten minutes drinking their coffee. Yuri takes a cigarette from his pocket and goes to light it.)

                    DMITRY
Don't do that, I got lucky before. I still have petrol on my clothes and I might go up in smoke this time. I am going to get out of these things and get a wash. I will see you in a while.

                    YURI
Okay...

(Dmitry walks out of the kitchen to go and find the bathroom.)

...Leave the water running, I will get straight in there after you.

Scene fades.

ACT I. SCENE 5

Thursday 16th October 10.30pm. It's dark in the streets of Moscow and the power is out everywhere. Alexander Ivanov and Viktor Popov emerge from an ally onto the corner of Valance Street. Ivanov is 34, 6ft 7 inches tall and has a muscular build, he is clean shaven and dressed in a grey boiler suit. Viktor is 57, 5ft 3 inches tall and has a skinny build. His complexion is ashen and his face is pockmarked. He walks with a limp, and looks ill. He is wearing a long grey Mac.

                    VIKTOR
See if you can get us some wheels while I phone Lidiya?

          (Alexander stubs a cigarette
          out on the pavement.)

                  ALEXANDER
Okay, be quick, this place is giving me the creeps.

          (Viktor crosses the road and
          enters a phone booth. He
          dials a number and inserts
          some coins.)

Scene fades.

ACT I. SCENE 6

In an apartment downtown in the poorer
quarters of Moscow, a yellow
wallmounted telephone is ringing. The
apartment is filled with cardboard
boxes and decorative glass swans,
deers, buffalo and rabbits. The walls
are painted red with yellow hammers
and sickles that are stencilled
ramdomly throughout the apartment.
Posters of cucumbers, bananas and
cherries hang in the living room
offering no visual aesthetic or
decorative appeal. For light, 10
neatly placed tea lights sit on the
mantelpiece and illuminate the room
with an eerie, spectral glow.
Flickering shadows of animals dance
along the walls, disappearing into the
windows and the darkness beyond. In
the middle of the apartment, a woman
called Lidiya sits eating a bowl of
ravioli and drinking cheap white wine.
She is 43, thin, blonde and anxious.
She stubbs out a cigarette, gets up,
and answers the phone nervously.

                    LIDIYA
Yes, who is it?

                    VIKTOR
Lidiya, it's Viktor. We need your
help?

LIDIYA
Viktor, what have you done? It's
been on the News all evening. All
those people dead. You have killed
39 innocent people. They are still
pulling more out of the rubble...

(Lidiya fumbles to light a
cigarette in her mouth.)

...They said you were arrested.
Where are you?

VIKTOR
Listen, I can't explain everything
now, it's too dangerous. We didn't
kill those people, they were not our
bombs. Listen Lidiya, Alexander and
I need our passports and some cash;
you will find them in the safe. Meet
us at the farmhouse at 7am, I will
explain everything then.

LIDIYA
I don't know if I can, I'm scared
Viktor.

VIKTOR
Lidiya, we need you. We are
innocent, I promise you. Please say
you will come.

(Lidiya is crying as she is
speaking.)

                    LIDIYA
Okay, I will come.

                    VIKTOR
Good girl. See you at seven. I love
you.

        *(Lidiya is now weeping hard
        and shaking.)*

                    LIDIYA
I love you too, Viktor.

        *(Viktor hangs up the phone
        and goes back out to the
        street. Alexander is waiting
        outside in a Maroon coloured
        Citroen 2CV6.)*

                    VIKTOR
What is this piece of junk?

                  ALEXANDER
It was in parking lot over there with
sign on window - *'Free to good home'*.
The keys were in the ignition, and
look...

        *(Alexander shows Viktor some
        money.)*

...there was a 1000 Rubles on the
seat. It is a sign Viktor.

(Viktor gets into the car.)

VIKTOR
Find us somewhere to park for a few
hours so we can get some sleep. We
are meeting Lidiya at the farmhouse
at 7am, she is bringing the cash and
our passports.

ALEXANDER
Good. I know an old junkyard we can
hide in until the morning.

(They drive away.)

Scene fades.

ACT I. SCENE 7

Thursday 16th October, 10.55pm.   At the farmhouse, Dmitry is in the living room. He is sitting on an orange sofa dressed in a cotton white bathrobe; he is studying the T.V. remote control. Yuri is walking through from the kitchen with a tray of food. He is dressed in a ladies pink satin bathrobe which is too small for him. He passes a plate to Dmitry and takes a seat.

                    YURI
Sorry, the food is not up to my usual standard, but I am at a loss without the right ingredients and my little gas burner.

        (Dmitry fiddles with the T.V.
        remote.)

                    DMITRY
That is alright, but it looks like you did a good job to me. Mince, potatoes, carrots and peas, just what the doctor ordered, and you even have a mint puree on the side.

        (Yuri takes a mouthful of
        food.)

                    YURI
It is all out of can, but beggars
can't be choosers. Turn on the T.V.
Dmitry, I want to see how much
trouble we are in.

                    DMITRY
That is what I have been trying to do
for past five minutes. It's too
complicated for me. Stupid thing, it
is rubbish. Why is it so
complicated?

                    YURI
Give it to me, I will sort it out.

        (Dmitry hands over the remote
        control.)

                    DMITRY
I guarantee it is not me, it is
broken.

        (The T.V. bursts into life.)

                    YURI
That's it. You were right Dmitry, it
was not you. The manufacturers of
this particular model of remote
control had cleverly disguised the
'on' button as the 'on' button - a
double bluff on their part; leading
the average person to press all of
the other buttons and arrive at the

conclusion it is broken.

                    DMITRY
I am tired Yuri, give me a break.
Turn it on to channel 5, the News is
about to start.

          (Yuri changes the channel to
          five and the news comes on.
          A lady Newscaster with black
          hair dressed in a red jumper
          is reporting.)

                    NEWSCASTER
...Thanks Bob. The top headlines
today...

          (Dramatic drum music and
          voice over.)

                    NARRATOR
...Your watching channel 5 News with
Katrina Chatovsky...

               KATRINA CHATOVSKY
Prime Minister Kantcoughsky, along
with 38 other diners attending the
commemorative banquet for the Russian
cosmonauts, Dmitry Usakov and Yuri
Chekov are believed to be dead
following an explosion at the Four
Seasons hotel earlier this evening.
Emergency services are continuing to
work through the night to uncover the

bodies buried in the rubble, but the loss of power throughout the sector is hindering the search. Inspector Plodovsky of the MPD had this to say...

> *(The picture changes to see an inspector from the Moscow Police Department; a small fat man with a black moustache. In the background, emergency workers search through the ruins of the Four Seasons hotel.)*

INSPECTOR PLODOVSKY

...Two men have been arrested in connection with the attack on the Four Seasons hotel. They are believed to be Alexander Ivanov and Viktor Popov of the terrorist action group O.F.E - The Organisation for Food Equality...

> *(Pictures of Alexander Ivanov and Viktor Popov are shown on screen alongside the Inspector.)*

...Shortly after the third explosion, Alexander Ivanov and Viktor Popov were found outside a local pawnbrokers handing out leaflets on food equality. They were arrested under the new terrorism act of 2015

and are now en route to a secure
location for questioning. Due to the
nature of the attack, armed forces
and military police were called in to
help with the arrest...

                    YURI
Do you see Dmitry, it is not our
pictures...

     (Yuri points at the T.V.)

...What was that stupid Sergeant
thinking of, mistaking us for those
two clowns. If he wasn't dead, I
could be quite mad at him.

                    DMITRY
Yuri, there is more going on here
than we realise. Let's see what else
the News has to say. We might learn
something.

     (They turn back to the T.V.)

               INSPECTOR PLODOVSKY
...The search for survivors is being
made all the more difficult due to
the loss of power in this sector and
the black dust which is continually
sweeping through the city. We've got
our hands full and it's a race
against time; people can only breathe
for so long under all that rubble.

(Returns to the studio.)

                KATRINA CHATOVSKY
...In other news tonight - The meteor
shower the Doomsday Soothsayers are
calling, the beginning to the end of
days. Earlier this evening, Moscow
was under fire from an unexpected
meteor shower. Hundreds of people
took to the streets of Moscow to
watch the spectacle, but were soon
forced back inside when large chunks
of metal began to fall causing
considerable damage to cars, property
and power lines. We are now going
live to our correspondent on the
scene...

        (On the T.V., A newscaster by
        the name of Anastasia
        Bedlumvich stands in front of
        St. Basil's Cathedral,
        Moscow.)

                ANASTASIA BEDLUMVICH
...As you can see, Moscow has no
power tonight and the city is in
total darkness. I'm standing outside
St. Basil's Cathedral with Sasha
Starovich, one of the unlucky
spectators to get caught in tonight's
meteor storm...

        (Anastasia addresses Sasha.)

...Sasha, what was it like being in the centre of this unusual celestial event?

SASHA
It was very frightening. At first I thought it was a firework display or somebody lost at sea, but then I remembered that we were a thousand kilometres from the Baltic and I went back to my original hypothesis - a firework display. It was only when my friend, Andrei, realised his jacket was on fire that I thought it must be something else.

ANASTASIA
What happened to your friend Andrei?

(Sasha points eastwards.)

SASHA
His jacket caught on fire and he ran off over there and fell down a manhole. I've been waiting here for him to come back up, but there has been no sign of him...

(A black cloud of dust covers Anastasia and Sasha and the screen goes blank before returning to the studio.)

NEWSCASTER
...We seem to be having technical difficulties with our report from Anastasia Bedlumvich and we have lost our link. In other news - A 79 year old Chinese woman as given birth to seven pork cutlets... Sorry, I meant to say Septuplets...

DMITRY
Turn it down Yuri. We've been harpooned into the trivial section of Channel 5 news where fantasy supersedes reality.

(Yuri mutes the T.V.)

YURI
Why do they always do that on the News? You can be watching somebody's limbs getting hacked-off by a machete in some African province one minute, and the next, you are watching the emergency services rescue a couple of old age pensioners from a double glazing salesman offering 20% off windows before September.

DMITRY
I know, it is stupid. Everyone knows that old age pensioners don't buy anything with just 20% off. It is a blatant misappropriation of vital Emergency Services at a time when

they might be needed elsewhere...

(Dmitry takes a last mouthful of food and puts his plate back on the tray.)

...That was pretty good Yuri. Did you make a dessert?

YURI
Actually I did. I opened a couple of cans of rice pudding, threw in some sultanas and dried apples, and grated some nutmeg on the top. I put it in the oven about 20 minutes ago, it should be ready in another ten.

DMITRY
Yuri, I have to say, if it wasn't for the creature comforts of home you have afforded us throughout this whole ordeal, I don't think I would have made it this far.

YURI
That is very kind of you to say so Dmitry...

(Yuri lights a cigarette.)

...Ahh, that is good...

(Yuri sits back in his chair puffing on his cigarette.)

...But I do know what you mean.

DMITRY
I don't suppose you came across any
bottles of vodka in the kitchen?

YURI
No, but I did notice that drinks
cabinet behind you.

(Dmitry turns to look.)

DMITRY
I thought that was an old Wireless
Set...

(Dmitry rises from his seat
and opens the cabinet.
Inside, bottles of various
alcoholic beverages can be
seen.)

...Jackpot! Things are looking up:
whisky, vodka, schnapps, Babycham,
Advocaat, Martini, Campari, coke,
lemonade and a soda siphon. What a
stroke of good fortune finding this
place in our moment of drought...

(Dmitry picks up the bottle
of vodka and pours a drink.)

...A veritable oasis in the desert.

Can I get you something Yuri?

                    YURI
Yes, I will have a whisky with a
splash of soda...

     (Dmitry hands Yuri the
     whisky.)

...Na Zdorovie!...

     (Yuri takes a sip of whisky
     and places the glass down on
     a small wooden coffee table
     and looks a little sombre.)

...Do you think we are safe here
Dmitry?

     (Dmitry refills his glass
     with vodka, takes a drink and
     smiles.)

                    DMITRY
Sure. That black dust is still
blowing outside and would have
covered our tracks completely by now.
It is like worst pea soup out there,
and it probably won't clear for a
couple of days. The emergency
services have their hands full
with...

     (Dmitry takes another drink
     and smiles.)

...with, emergencies, and nobody
knows we are here but us...

> (Dmitry takes a seat and puts
> his feet up.)

...Even the powers that be are
probably scratching their heads in
all this chaos.

                    YURI
Why do you think the army thought we
were terrorist suspects?

                    DMITRY
I don't know, but something else is
in operation that we are not aware
of.

> (Dmitry tops up Yuri's
> glass.)

                    YURI
Thank you. Like what?

                    DMITRY
I am not certain, but tonight's
bombing has changed everything. We
both know there has been much civil
unrest in the last couple of years,
and no one is particularly fond of
our current government, and...

> (Dmitry takes a drink.)

                    YURI
And what?

                    DMITRY
And, it might have been more of a
planned set of events than we think.
Take the bombing of the hotel.

                    YURI
What about it?

                    DMITRY
It might be nothing, but, do you not
find it strange how quickly the
emergency services and the army were
at the scene?

    (Yuri sits up.)

                    YURI
Come to think of it, yes. I could
hear police sirens and low rumble of
trucks on street before bombs even
went off.

                    DMITRY
Exactly.

    *(Yuri lights another
    cigarette and takes a puff.)*

                    YURI
But we did crash land in an alien
shuttle craft moments before...

     (Yuri rubs his chin.)

...What do you think it means?

                  DMITRY
It means, the powers that be, knew
all about the bombs long before
tonight's attack. In fact, the way
that hotel came down was more like a
controlled demolition; straight down
in its own footprint. That kind of
levelling of a building takes expert
knowledge and correct placement of
explosives over a few days. I don't
believe a couple of campaigners for
food equality are responsible for
that atrocity, especially when their
M.O. is placing fart cushions on
public buses.

     (Yuri looks pensive.)

                    YURI
So, what is going on?

                  DMITRY
I think we were at the beginning of a
coup d'état and somebody pulled the
pin out of the grenade before an
inevitable downfall and overthrow of

the government could start. The
banquet at the Four Seasons hotel was
announced by Prime Minister
Kantcoughsky as soon as there was a
report saying the *Space Station* had
exploded. A hotel like the Four
Seasons would have needed several
days notice, if not weeks to book a
function like that, yet Kantcoughsky
is talking about a banquet and its
location minutes after we are
pronounced dead. Knowing that
scumbag, he probably sent out the
invitations a month ago.

> *(Yuri rubs his head.)*

                    YURI
You really know your stuff Dmitry, I
have a hard time remembering whether
I use the pink toothbrush or the
green one. The wife usually shouts
through from the kitchen when she
hears the sink tap running.

> *(Dmitry takes a drink.)*

                   DMITRY
I hope I am wrong, but I think we
have witnessed a false flag operation
in progress.

                    YURI
Is that when you have a flag in your

pocket and you get chased around the playground until your flag is captured.

                    DMITRY
No, that is a child's game called 'Tag Flag', this is much more serious. Why would Kantcoughsky chase children round a playground?...

        (Dmitry looks at Yuri incredulously.)

...A false flag operation is when a government commits an act of terrorism against itself in order to blame it on somebody else. Somebody like, *'El liga de hombres en contra grueso negro bigotes'*, or as in this case, *The Organisation for Food Equality*. They have been a constant annoyance to Kantcoughsky throughout his administration with their perpetual campaigning for food equality for the people of Russia. Kantcoughsky doesn't want food equality, he wants it all for himself.

        (Yuri rubs his head again.)

                    YURI
Pour me another drink Dmitry, my head is hurting. How do we figure in all this mess?

                    DMITRY
Well, if my hypothesis is correct,
Prime Minister Kantcoughsky knew in
advance the *Space Station* was going
to blow up and that a function would
be taking place at the Four Seasons
hotel a few days later...

        (*Dmitry paces a little.*)

...Most of the council for the
federation would be attending the
banquet, so it is a good place to
plant a bomb if you wish to take out
your opposition. Now, you have an
excellent opportunity for
misdirection, by laying the blame on
some food activists that have been in
the public eye over the last year...

        (*Dmitry stops pacing.*)

...It makes a lot of sense Yuri.
With Viktor Popov and Alexander
Ivanov arrested for the bombing, the
government have already cast the
blame on a vexing, troublesome
faction and removed any suspicion
from themselves...

        (*Dmitry starts to pace
        again.*)

...This means Kantcoughsky is a
definite king pin behind these

events. We shouldn't believe he is
dead just yet, but in hiding...

> (Dmitry stumbles over to the
> drinks cabinet and grabs a
> bottle of schnapps. He walks
> back to his seat and pours
> himself a drink.)

...If Kantcoughsky should somehow
appear from beneath the debris at the
hotel, possibly with another
survivor, he would be heralded as a
hero. With the vote coming up in a
month's time, he would be favourite
for re-election - No question.
Especially when you consider that
most of the opposing candidates for
consideration were at that hotel. If
you are dead, there is a good chance
you won't get a vote. So, by process
of elimination, Kantcoughsky would
win by default.

                    YURI
There is a lot of supposition in your
argument Dmitry, but it is plausible.
You will either turn out to be
correct and prove your hypothesis, or
just another drunk with crazy ideas.

> (Dmitry points at Yuri with a
> wandering finger.)

                    DMITRY
Huh, crazy am I. After that soup
scandal last year, Kantcoughsky had
no chance of re-election this time
around. He was well behind in the
polls. With the *Communist
Confederate Front* out of the picture,
the only opposing party is the
Liberal Black Cats, and nobody votes
for them, they are insane.

                     YURI
What soup scandal?

                    DMITRY
Do you not remember in the News, they
were calling it 'SOUPGATE'.

                     YURI
SOUPGATE? No, I don't remember
anything about last year, I was too
busy with my Uncle Baggetsky and his
bakery fiasco. I know nothing of a
soup scandal. What was that all
about?

                    DMITRY
Kantcoughsky was stealing cans of
soup from the canteen store cupboard
in the Kremlin building and selling
them to a black-market trader. They
say it was big business, he was
getting away with 60-70 cans of
tomato soup a week. Each can could

fetch up to 200 Rubles; if they were
still sealed, as much as 400. I tell
you, he has always been a slippery
character, and it would not surprise
me if he crawls out of that bomb site
without a scratch...

    (Dmitry pours himself another
    drink.)

...What was the problem with your
uncle's bakery?

    (Dmitry takes a long drag on
    a cigarette.)

            YURI
It was nothing really, he got into
trouble with the local constabulary
after selling a bad batch of bread.

          DMITRY
It is not like police to get involved
in the quality of a bakers loaf.
What happened exactly, too much
yeast?

            YURI
It was just a mistake, that is all,
it could have happened to anyone...

    (Yuri takes a puff on his
    cigarette.)

...He was completely innocent of any wrong doing, it was just an accident.

                    DMITRY
What did he do Yuri?

                    YURI
Well, I better start from beginning. My Uncle Baggetsky had been suffering a long time with rheumatoid arthritis, especially in his wrists. Every day it was getting a little harder to need dough for bread, so he went to doctor for some help. The doctor said it was an age related ailment and that the type of work my uncle did only exacerbated the problem. The doctor said there was no cure and suggested retirement...

        *(Yuri gathers up the dishes
        and starts to walk to the
        kitchen.)*

...This was not a word my uncle was fond of...

        *(Yuri places the dishes on
        the side and checks in the
        oven for the rice pudding.
        He takes it out of the oven
        and dishes it up into two
        bowls and returns to the
        living room. He passes one
        to Dmitry.)*

                    DMITRY
Thanks Yuri. What about police?

                     YURI
I am getting to that. After his
visit to the doctor, he struggled on
for another week at the bakery and
was about to admit defeat, when
something happened.

        (Dmitry is spooning the rice
        pudding into his mouth like a
        wild animal.)

                    DMITRY
What happened Yuri?

                     YURI
He went to the pub on the corner of
Hamlet street - 'The Fish and The
Frog Inn'. There, over several pints
of brown ale, he told an old friend
about his plight and the end of his
livelihood. His friend suggested a
homeopathic remedy that he had heard
of in the form of a herbal plant. He
told my uncle that in such cases as
his, where traditional medicines had
failed to reduce pain in the joints,
there had been excellent results in
the reduction of joint pain when
smoking this herbal remedy. His
friend went on to say, that if he was
interested in trying it out, he would

ask a local grower to pop past his bakery and drop off a sample. My Uncle felt he had nothing to lose and told his friend to send round the herbal plant grower...

> *(Dmitry takes a last mouthful of rice pudding and puts the bowl on the table.)*

...Was that a good pudding Dmitry?

                    DMITRY
Yes, that little bit of nutmeg really gave it a boost, a bit of a zing - very tasty...

> *(Dmitry takes another drink of vodka. His speech is starting to slur.)*

...Yuri, police?

                    YURI
Yes. Well early next morning, my uncle opened his bakery and started to make the dough for bread. He was not feeling very well, he had had a little too much to drink at *'The Fish and The Frog Inn'* and his head was pounding. At 5.30am, a young man walked into the bakery with a bag under his arm. It turned out to be herbal plant grower that his friend spoke of night before. After a

general conversation about benefits of herb, the man leaves bakery without bag.

                    DMITRY
So your uncle bought some of the herb?

                     YURI
Not just some, but all. After he had smoked a couple of cigarettes, he started to feel great and was working like a man of 21. In his euphoric state he began to sing Russian folks songs and do a Cossack dance around the bakery. By mistake, he knocked the bag of herbs into bread mix...

        (Yuri lights a cigarette and
        takes a puff.)

...He sold over 200 hundred loaves that day to many of his best customers. Fortunately for him, the herb had a beneficial effect on the majority of his patrons with most of them having a productive weekend and a general sense of well-being. Unfortunately, about 10% of them ended up in hospital or jail; one of them was even discovered a week later on a salvage ship en route to Los Mochis, Mexico.

                    DMITRY
Your uncle had purchased Cannabis?

                    YURI
He had no knowledge of narcotics, he
had been a baker from the age of 10;
yeast and flour was his thing. He
thought it was herb like basil.

                    DMITRY
Did he go to jail for distribution of
a class B drug?

                    YURI
No, the prosecution failed to prove
their case against him and he got off
with a 100 hours of community
service. The judge felt my uncle had
done irreparable damage to his
business and showed him leniency due
to his age. The judge felt a prison
sentence would be of no benefit to a
man of my uncles years.

                    DMITRY
How old was your uncle?

                    YURI
He was only 92.

                    DMITRY
92? What kind of community service
did they give him?

YURI

It was nothing taxing, it was mostly
at the local vicarage, planting bulbs
and painting, that sort of thing.
The judge felt it was an appropriate
recompense under the circumstances.

DMITRY

What do you mean?

YURI

Well, the vicar and his wife had been
loyal customers of my uncle, and that
day, was no exception, they had
bought their usual bloomer loaf and
sat outside for afternoon tea, bread
and jam. The next morning the vicar
conducted his sermon from the pulpit
as usual, except he was not wearing
any clothes. His wife had taken it
upon herself to walk around the town
in her nightdress painting all of the
cars with a yellow stripe. Later
that day, they were both arrested and
charged with crimes of vandalism,
lewd and insidious behaviour and
resisting arrest.

DMITRY

I take it your uncle has now retired?

YURI

Yes. The bakery was taken over by my
cousin Vasily, but it is not the

same. Vasily has no passion for food
and his bread is heavy like house
brick. He will never be the baker my
uncle was.

                    DMITRY
Shame, but your uncle deserves a rest
at 92. Perhaps your cousin Vasily
will improve with time.

                    YURI
I don't think so, this is the third
bakery a relative as given him, the
other two went bankrupt after 6
Months...

        (Yuri looks at the T.V. and
        jumps out of his seat.)

...Dmitry, look!

        (They both stare at the T.V.
        An army truck is pulling a
        large trailer and driving
        away from the ruins of the
        Four Seasons hotel. The
        trailer is covered with a
        tarpaulin and conceals what
        is underneath.)

                    DMITRY
What do you think is underneath that
cover Yuri?

                    YURI
I am not the best person to recognise
a covered shape, but even I would say
it bears an uncanny resemblance to
that of a large oval. If I was to
put two and two together, I would say
that is alien shuttle craft on way to
secret location.

                   DMITRY
I would say you are right.

                    YURI
All of our evidence is disappearing
Dmitry, before long we will have no
proof of anything. What are we going
to do?

                   DMITRY
It is a shame we lost video camera
and shuttle craft, but as long as we
are alive, the truth will be known...

     (Dmitry pours Yuri another
     drink and then himself.)

...Our best plan of action for now is
to have a good night's sleep and
think of our next move in the
morning.

                    YURI
You are right, a fresh perspective on
things always brings some clarity.

DMITRY
I personally prefer a nice Bordeaux.

YURI
I said clarity, not claret.

DMITRY
Shame, I fancied a nice drop of
something different.

Scene fades.

ACT I. SCENE 8

Friday 17th October, 2025.   3.30am, Downtown, Moscow. Inside Lidiya's apartment the light is fading and grows dimmer with each passing hour. Only 5 of the original 10 tea lights remain true to their 8 hour promise and even they are unlikely to go the distance. Lidiya is sprawled out on her sofa and is fast asleep. Her bottle of white wine is emtpy and her bowl of ravioli unfinished.   An explosion occurs in the other room and her apartment door is blown from its hinges. Seconds later, armed police with sniffer dogs enter her living quarters. She wakes with a start.

POLICEMAN 1
Go, go ,go!

*(8 armed policemen, dressed
in black, surround Lidiya on
her sofa. 4 other policemen,
2 with dogs, search the
apartment. A policeman talks
on his radio.)*

POLICEMAN 2
Area secured, suspect detained. Repeat, suspect detained.

                    POLICEMAN 3
There's nobody else here. The rooms
are clear.

        (A small man wearing a dark
        blue suit and tie enters the
        apartment. He is clean
        shaven and his hair is gelled
        back. In his left hand, he
        holds a freshly lit
        cigarette. He is Lieutenant
        Jess Tapovich from the MPD.)

                    LT. TAPOVICH
Where is she?

                    POLICEMAN 2
This way lieutenant.

        (The lieutenant walks over to
        Lidiya, who is shaking
        nervously on her sofa. She
        sits up and wipes her eyes,
        pulls a multi-coloured
        crocheted blanket over
        herself and looks up at the
        lieutenant.)

                    LIDIYA
What's happening?

                    LT. TAPOVICH
You are under arrest for conspiracy
to commit murder.

                    LIDIYA
Murder?

                  LT. TAPOVICH
At last count, 38 to be precise.

       *(Lidiya reaches for a
       cigarette. Policeman 2 talks
       to the lieutenant in
       private.)*

                  POLICEMAN 2
There is nobody else here, but we did
find a bag on the kitchen counter.
There is a large sum of money inside
and two passports - Viktor Popov and
Alexander Ivanov.

       *(The lieutenant looks at
       Lidiya.)*

                  LT. TAPOVICH
Lidiya, I need to ask you a few
questions. How you choose to answer
these questions is up to you, but be
advised, failing to cooperate with
the police during an investigation is
a serious offence and can carry a
maximum sentence of life
imprisonment. Add to that, the
conspiracy charges, and you could be
looking at a minimum of 52 years in
prison. So, think carefully before
you answer my questions...

*(The lieutenant stubs out his
cigarette and lets out a
final puff.)*

...Do you know the whereabouts of
Viktor Popov and Alexander Ivanov?

LIDIYA
No, why would I. I am just a poor
glass menagerie manufacturer in a
world of plastic.

*(The lieutenant shows Lidiya
two passports with the names
Viktor Popov and Alexander
Ivanov.)*

LT. TAPOVICH
Then how do you explain their
passports in your apartment with a
large bag of money?

LIDIYA
They've been staying here the last
few days.

LT. TAPOVICH
Is that when you put together your
plan to blow up the hotel?

LIDIYA
What? No! I had nothing to do with
that. I was just helping them out
with folding leaflets for our next

campaign.

                    LT. TAPOVICH
C'mon Lidiya, do you think we are
stupid?...

          *(Policeman 2 walks over to
          the lieutenant and slips him
          a piece of folded paper with
          a picture of hungry children
          on it.)*

...Folding leaflets, doesn't seem to
be a very productive way to spend
your time?

          *(Lidiya puffs her cigarette
          and blows the smoke at the
          lieutenant's face.)*

                    LIDIYA
Maybe not for a big shot like you,
but for us poor plebs, it is a way of
saving money. A Printer will charge
a lot of money for that service...

          *(Lidiya picks up the wine
          bottle, sees it is empty and
          puts it back on the table.)*

...and we can only afford small
batches.

                    LT. TAPOVICH
If you are so poor, where did that
bag of money come from?

                    LIDIYA
That is not mine, it is Viktor's, he
just sold his van to pay for campaign
print job. It is hardly a big bag of
money. If you check the currency you
will see it is all 5's. There is
only 70,000 rubles in there. He sold
it to a young painter and decorator
who had been saving up his money to
get a vehicle. The money was from
his piggybank. If you look in the
bottom of the bag you will find a
bill of sale and broken pieces of
porcelain.

        (Policeman 2 checks out the
        bag.)

                    POLICEMAN 2
She is right lieutenant, they're all
fives.

        (The lieutenant looks at
        policeman 2.)

                    LT. TAPOVICH
What about the bill of sale and the
broken porcelain?

                    POLICEMAN 2
Also there, I can just make out a
snout.

        (The lieutenant looks back
        towards Lidiya.)

                    LT. TAPOVICH
Okay, so you're telling the truth
about the money, but that doesn't let
you off the hook. Last night,
approximately at 10.30pm, you
received a phone call from a payphone
on the corner of Valance street. The
conversation lasted 1 minute 12
seconds, who was it that called you,
and what did you speak about?

                    LIDIYA
Last night? I can't remember. It
must have been a wrong number.

                    LT. TAPOVICH
Can't remember? Wrong number? Quit
stalling. We know it was Viktor,
we've got him on C.C.T.V walking out
of the phone booth on the corner of
Valance street at 10.33pm, and we
know he phoned this number. Now,
what did you speak about?

        (Lidiya fumbles with a packet
        of cigarettes. Her hands are
        shaking.)

                    LIDIYA
He needed money and his passport.

        *(The lieutenant lights her
        cigarette.)*

                  LT. TAPOVICH
And how is he suppose to get the
money and passports? Is he coming
here, or do you have to meet him some
place?

                    LIDIYA
His late father has a farm out in the
country, I was going to meet him and
Alexander there at 7am this morning.

                  LT. TAPOVICH
How far is this farm from here?

                    LIDIYA
It is about an hour's drive.

                  LT. TAPOVICH
Get some clothes on, you are taking
us there.

Scene fades.

ACT 2. SCENE 1

Friday 17th October, 6.42am. Inside
the farmhouse, Yuri and Dmitry are
fast asleep. Yuri is still wearing
his pink satin bathrobe and is slumped
over an armchair in the living room.
Dmitry is sprawled out across the sofa
clutching an empty bottle of Babycham
and is still wearing his bathrobe.
Outside, the sun is starting to rise
and it's the beginning of a beautiful
day, the sky is clear and the black
dust has gone. A cockerel exits from
a shed and walks into the farm court
yard and crows - 'cock-a-doodle-doo'.
Yuri wakes up.

                    YURI
What is that noise?...

        (Yuri moves from his twisted
        position and sits up. He
        wipes his face.)

...Oh, my head, it is coming off...

        (Yuri grabs a cigarette from
        his packet, lights it and
        takes a draw.)

...Dmitry, wake up!

        (Dmitry moves a little.)

                    DMITRY
I told you Mama, not again, they are
horrible to me, even that Joey
Krispin's a bully. The fire is too
hot...

        (Dmitry starts to move
        restlessly.)

...They won't find the gold Mama,
it's buried in the river bed.

                    YURI
Dmitry, stop that mumbling and wake
up!

                    DMITRY
What?

                    YURI
Wake up!

        (Dmitry moves from his lying
        position and sits up.)

                    DMITRY
Where am I? What is this place? You
are not my Mama.

                    YURI
Dmitry, you idiot. It is me, Yuri.

We are at farmhouse, remember?

                    DMITRY
Yuri! Oh, I remember. Oh, no. I
can't feel my face.

                    YURI
I am not surprised, you had a lot to
drink last night. At one point you
were even licking the label on the
bottle.

                    DMITRY
What time is it?

                    YURI
It's a little before seven.

        (Dmitry begins to move and
        stand up. Outside a car
        pulls into the driveway.)

                    DMITRY
What's that?

        (Dmitry looks at Yuri.)

                    YURI
It sounded like a car.

        (A strip of light drifts into
        the living room through a
        crack in the boards covering

*the window. Dmitry rushes
over to the window and looks
through the crack in the
boards.)*

DMITRY
It's a car. I can't see very well.
It's an old red Citroen...

*(Dmitry wipes his eyes to see
better.)*

...There are two men getting out.

YURI
What are they doing? Are they coming
up to the house.

DMITRY
No. They are just chatting and
looking down the lane.

*(Yuri moves closer to
Dmitry.)*

What do they look like?

DMITRY
I can only see one of them clearly.
He is a tall fellow, must be 6'7 at
least. White skin and blonde hair.

(Yuri moves behind Dmitry.)

                    YURI
Let me see?

                   DMITRY
Wait. I can see the other fellow
now. Small ashen looking guy 5'2
maybe, pockmarked skin. Now I can
see them clearly, they remind me of
somebody. Can't think who, but I
have definitely seem them before.

                    YURI
Let me see?

        (Dmitry moves away from the
        window and Yuri looks through
        the crack. He turns back to
        face Dmitry with a look of
        dread on his face.)

                   DMITRY
What is it, what is wrong?

                    YURI
You idiot! What do you mean you
think you have seem them before?
That's is Viktor Popov and Alexander
Ivanov. We've got to get out of
here!

                   DMITRY
Who?

                    YURI
Who? Dmitry, you drink too much.
The terrorists from the O.F.E.
Y'know the fart cushion guys.

                    DMITRY
What?...

        (Dmitry looks through the
        crack in the boards again.)

...You're right. What are they doing
here?

        (Another car pulls into the
        drive, an orange fiat 126.
        Lidiya gets out with a bag.)

...Somebody else is here, another
car. A woman is getting out. She
has a black bag. She is giving it to
Viktor.

        (Yuri is walking about the
        living room anxiously.)

                    YURI
Let's get out of here Dmitry.

                    DMITRY
What are you talking about, we are
not even dressed...

        (Dmitry looks down the lane.

A green van is approaching at high speed. It is a UAZ-452 military police vehicle.

...The military police are coming.

                    YURI
What shall we do?

> *(The police van stops quickly and four armed policemen jump out. Lt. Tapovich follows shortly afterwards.)*

                    DMITRY
Wait. I don't think they are here for us.

> *(Dmitry looks on at the action. Viktor and Alexander are placed under arrest and put in the back of the van.)*

                    YURI
I can't stand this, what is happening?

                    DMITRY
Yuri, shut up before somebody hears you. It's alright, they have arrested Viktor and that Alexander guy. A cop in a blue suit is talking to the woman, it looks like she is getting some money from him. I think

she is leaving. Yes, she has got
back in her car. She has left...

(Dmitry adjusts his position
to see better.)

...A policeman is approaching the red
Citroen. He has a Jerry can, he is
pouring petrol over the car.

(Dmitry looks back at Yuri.)

YURI
What?

DMITRY
Strange, he just walked away...

(Dmitry looks back through
the crack.)

...No, he has thrown something. The
car is on fire. They are leaving
Yuri...

(The armed policemen and Lt.
Tapovich return to their van
and leave with Viktor and
Alexander.)

...They have gone Yuri.

YURI
What a relief. I don't know how much

more of this I can take. It is very
bad for the digestion. If you will
excuse me for a minute.

> *(Outside the farmhouse the
> Citroen explodes and small
> fires burst out in every
> direction. Dmitry takes one
> final look outside and sits
> back on the sofa. On the
> T.V. the 7 O'clock news is
> just starting. Dmitry turns
> up the sound. A small drum
> roll is heard, followed by 5
> notes from a trumpet.)*

NEWS NARRATOR
This is the 7 O'clock news with Vicki
Volkov.

> *(A woman in her 30's, blonde
> hair, glasses and a lavender
> dress appears on the T.V.)*

VICKI VOLKOV
Hello, I'm Vicki Volkov. Fire
fighters and emergency services have
been working through the night
searching for possible survivors from
yesterday's bombing at the Four
Seasons hotel. So far, 39 people,
including the leader of the
federation for communism, Lenny Marx,
have been pronounced dead. The
search continues for Prime Minister

Kantcoughsky and other members of The Federation Council, but as the hours pass, the chances of finding them alive decrease dramatically...

    (Dmitry goes to the kitchen and makes Yuri and himself some coffee. After a couple of minutes, he returns to the sofa in the living room with the drinks.)

...A report is just coming in from the bomb site. Emergency Services have found somebody alive...

    (Dmitry drinks some coffee. Yuri returns to the living room.)

                  DMITRY
Yuri, I made you some Coffee.

                   YURI
Thanks, I am a bit thirsty. What's happening in the News.

    (Yuri looks at the T.V.)

                  DMITRY
It appears they have found someone at the bomb site.

VICKY VOLKOV
...Reporting live at the scene is
Anastasia Bedlumvich...

> (The screen goes back and
> forth between the News Anchor
> and the reporter.)

...Anastasia, can you tell us what's
happening just now?

ANASTASIA BEDLUMVICH
As you can see behind me, fire
fighters are waiting for this crane
to move some rubble from a location
at the back of the hotel...

> (A crane is lifting big
> pieces of concrete from the
> bomb site and putting them
> onto the back of a dumper
> truck.)

...Approximately 15 minutes ago,
emergency service workers reported
some voices coming from the toilet
block of the hotel. It is believed
that this section of the hotel is
largely untouched and structurally
sound, so the possibility of more
survivors now seems likely...

> (Behind the reporter, fire
> fighters are pulling two
> people out of the rubble.

*The camera zooms into the
area to look at the scene.
Prime Minister Kantcoughsky
and Olga Usakov emerge from
the rubble. They look
surprisingly clean for their
ordeal.)*

                    DMITRY
Yuri, are you seeing this?

        (Dmitry spills his coffee.)

                    YURI
I am seeing it, but I am not
believing it. Who is that with
Kantcoughsky?

                    DMITRY
I would recognise that mug anywhere,
no one has a countenance like my
Olga. Her face is the colour of
pumpkin and her teeth are as white as
cotton.

                    YURI
So, your wife went to memorial after
all.

                    DMITRY
It would seem so...

        *(Dmitry takes a drink of his
        coffee.)*

...Look! Here they come.

ANASTASIA BEDLUMVICH
Prime Minister? Prime Minister?...

> (Prime Minister Kantcoughsky
> and Olga Usakov are being led
> to the back of an ambulance.
> They are given some water and
> a blanket.)

...Are you glad to be out of the
wreckage and alive?

P.M. KANTCOUGHSKY
That is a stupid question. What
would you think if I said no?

> (Kantcoughsky drinks some
> water. Olga sits by his
> side.)

ANASTASIA BEDLUMVICH
I would think you were suffering from
concussion...

> (Anastasia moves closer to
> the Prime Minister.)

...Perhaps a slightly more difficult
question. Can you tell us how you
and Mrs. Usakov seemed to have no
injuries to your person and
practically no dust on your clothes?

(*Kantcoughsky looks up and
then at Olga.*)

P.M. KANTCOUGHSKY
Well...

(*Kantcoughsky pauses for a
minute.*)

...We were in the toilet block, and
that section of the hotel was largely
untouched by the explosion.

ANASTASIA BEDLUMVICH
You are talking about the Men's
toilet block, because as I understand
it, the women's was totally
destroyed.

P.M. KANTCOUGHSKY
Of course. Why would I be in the
ladies?

ANASTASIA BEDLUMVICH
You wouldn't, but why is Mrs. Usakov
here, she should've been killed.
Surely she wasn't in the Men's room
with you?

(*Kantcoughsky keeps looking
at Olga.*)

No. I met her out in the corridor.
I was on my way to see where my

waiter was. I had dropped my fish
and requested another.

              ANASTASIA BEDLUMVICH
What made you drop your fish?

        *(Yuri sits down next to
        Dmitry and takes a sip of
        coffee.)*

                  YURI
This should be interesting.

              P.M. KANTCOUGHSKY
I can't remember. That is not the
point, the point is I met Mrs. Usakov
in the corridor. Isn't that right
Olga?

                OLGA USAKOV
Yes, that's right Snookums, 7.52pm.
Just like you said.

        *(Kantcoughsky goes red in the
        face.)*

              P.M. KANTCOUGHSKY
I think that is enough questions for
now.

              ANASTASIA BEDLUMVICH
Prime Minister, why did Mrs. Usakov
call you 'Snookums'?

                    P.M. KANTCOUGHSKY
Did she, I didn't notice. Now if you
will excuse me, I have been waiting
on this man.

        *(A pizza delivery van pulls
        up next to the ambulance. A
        young man gets out carrying a
        pizza box and walks over to
        Kantcoughsky.)*

                    PIZZA MAN
Are you Kantcoughsky?

                    P.M. KANTCOUGHSKY
Yes, that's me.

                    PIZZA MAN
You ordered the pepperoni pie with
extra cheese, green peppers and
onions - no olives?

                    P.M. KANTCOUGHSKY
Yes, that sounds right.

        *(The pizza delivery man hands
        over the pizza pie.)*

                    PIZZA MAN
That'll be 2000 rubles please?

        *(Kantcoughsky hands over some
        money.)*

> P.M. KANTCOUGHSKY
Here, keep the change...

> *(Kantcoughsky opens the box
> and takes a bite.)*

...Olga, take a piece, it's very
nice; but be careful it's hot.

> *(The pizza delivery man
> returns to his van and drives
> off.)*

> ANASTASIA BEDLUMVICH
Prime Minister, when did you order
that pizza?

> OLGA
He ordered it last night if you must
know...

> *(Olga takes a bite out of the
> pizza.)*

...Before we left to go to the
hotel...

> *(Olga takes another bite.)*

... Why, did you think he ordered it
from under the rubble?...

> *(Olga starts to laugh and
> addresses Kantcoughsky.)*

...Some people are so stupid!

(Kantcoughsky looks up from his pizza.)

P.M. KANTCOUGHSKY
Olga, be quiet.

ANASTASIA BEDLUMVICH
Prime Minister, I have just one more question. I am sure all of the people at home would be interested as well. Why did you order a pizza last night to be delivered at this location at 7.10am today?

(Kantcoughsky looks up at Anastasia.)

P.M. KANTCOUGHSKY
Erm, there is my car. I would like to chat more, but duty calls. Olga you get in first.

(Olga and Prime Minister Kantcoughsky get into a black limousine and drive away. Dmitry is just staring at the T.V.)

ANASTASIA BEDLUMVICH
...This has been Anastasia Bedlumvich with channel 5 News.

*(Dmitry turns down the T.V.
with the remote control and
walks about the living room.)*

DMITRY

I can't believe it. I have been so
blind...

*(Dmitry throws his hands in
the air.)*

...Here I have been filling your head
with convoluted theories about the
machinations of our government and
how unscrupulous and disingenuous
they can be, and all the time...

*(Dmitry opens a bottle of
Babycham.)*

...And all the time, my own wife has
been having relations with the very
person who is behind this whole
affair...

(Dmitry drinks the Babycham.)

...right under my nose. I thought
all this time, the arguments and the
constant complaining about our
relationship and how unhappy she was,
was all my fault...

(Dmitry sits down.)

...But here she is, sleeping with the enemy, and happy as a crow with fresh road kill. I haven't even been dead 5 minutes and she's moved on.

                    YURI
Dmitry, don't take it so hard. You knew your relationship was over. You said yourself that we were never home. Y'know what they say, 'When the cat is away, the mice eat the cheese'. That is a very true proverb.

     *(Dmitry looks at the floor
     depressed.)*

                    DMITRY
What? Yes, cheese...

     (Dmitry stares at Yuri.)

...Pizza!

                    YURI
What about it?

                    DMITRY
Pizza, Yuri. How did Kantcoughsky know he was going to need pizza at 7.10am today?

                    YURI
What?

                    DMITRY
He must have known that the Four
Seasons hotel was going to be blown
up and that he would be rescued at
7am this morning. He had already
ordered the pizza the night before.
He is behind all of this. C'mon
Yuri, let's get going.

     *(Yuri points at his and
     Dmitry's attire.)*

                    YURI
Perhaps, we should find something a
bit warmer to wear.

     *(Dmitry looks at his
     bathrobe.)*

                    DMITRY
Yes, perhaps we should. Let's have a
look in the bedroom for a wardrobe.

Scene fades.

ACT 2, SCENE 2

London, United Kingdom, 7.25am, Friday 17th October, 2025. George London crosses the street and enters the headquarters of the British Secret Service MI5. He swipes a card in a turnstile, waves at a security guard and enters a lift. Inside the lift he enters a code on a wall panel:20HO7a69X. The wall behind him disappears to reveal a staircase leading down. He uses the staircase and comes to a door, he knocks once, then three short taps, then opens the door. Inside, he is greeted by the head of MI5, Sir Lucas B. Windbag. Sir Windbag is a portly man in his 50's wearing a light brown suit and tie with milk bottle bottom spectacles and a thin brown moustache.

LUCAS B. WINDBAG
Ah, London, there you are. Been waiting on your report. I hope you have some encouraging news to share, lord knows we need it. Terrible business this *Space Station* thing, what?

GEORGE LONDON
Yes, frightful sir, but it would seem we have a much bigger problem now.

(*Sir Lucas B. Windbag puts a* Bent Rhodesian *pipe in his mouth and lights it with a match from a book of matches advertising the* 'Bunny Club'. *A cloud of smoke momentarily extrudes his face, then drifts out the window.*)

SIR LUCAS B. WINDBAG
What's that you say, a bigger problem? Bigger than our involvement in the concealment of the Dome and that alien space ship?

(*Sir Lucas B. Windbag finishes his sentence with a smile. George London looks on concerned.*)

GEORGE LONDON
Yes, I am afraid so, sir. You see, the Dome has vanished and the spaceship has gone.

SIR LUCAS B. WINDBAG
Oh, I see. Bit of a turn up for the books, what? Gone you say, gone where exactly?

GEORGE LONDON
Have you not seen the news this morning, sir?

SIR LUCAS B. WINDBAG
News? Good lord no. Nothing worse
than watching the news over
breakfast, upsets the digestion. I
find a good cartoon and a stiff drink
is the best way to start the day,
gets the old chuckle muscles going
and soothes the brain. Now if
there's nothing more, I have to get
down to the bookies. Had a bit of a
wager on the ponies yesterday and
'Soldier Boy' came in first place at
25-1.

GEORGE LONDON
But I haven't given you my report
yet.

SIR LUCAS B. WINDBAG
Haven't you? Sorry I'd thought we'd
finished...

*(George London looks on in
dismay.)*

...Well, go on lad, what you waiting
for?

GEORGE LONDON
Yes, well...

*(George London looks at Sir
Lucas B. Windbag puffing away
on his pipe.)*

...Following the disappearance of the invisible barrier last night...

SIR LUCAS B. WINDBAG
What's that you say, invisible what?

(George London smiles and points to the ceiling.)

GEORGE LONDON
Y'know sir, the old cupola in the sky.

LUCAS B. WINDBAG
What? Cup of who? In what sky?

GEORGE LONDON
The Dome, sir.

SIR LUCAS B. WINDBAG
Then why didn't you bally well say so in the first place.

GEORGE LONDON
Yes, sir. Following the disappearance of the Dome last night at 7.37pm, the observatory at Parkhurst captured some disturbing images with its telescope.

SIR LUCAS B. WINDBAG
Did they, by Jove. Yes, well, we all

know what that's like. I remember as
a boy looking at the constellation
Cassiopeia through the old *Telstar
345* series when it slipped off the
tripod and focused on the local vicar
in his house. That was a ghastly
sight I can tell you. There he was,
as large as life, parading around his
living room with a pink dress on,
pink gloves up to his elbows, white
pearls around his neck and a feather
hat on his head...

(*Sir Lucas B. Windbag starts
to gesticulate.*)

...And to add a touch of decadence to
the scene, a glass of '54 Beaujolais
in his right hand spilling all over
the carpet as if it was water. I ask
you, wouldn't that sort of thing scar
you for life?

GEORGE LONDON
Yes, I suppose it might invalidate
any religious inclinations one might
have if they were that way inclined,
but it seems harmless enough, and of
course, it would all depend on the
particular shade of pink he was
wearing...

SIR LUCAS B. WINDBAG
What?... Quite, quite so. Yes, I
never thought of that. Where were

we?

                    GEORGE LONDON
The Parkhurst Observatory, sir.

                  SIR LUCAS B. WINDBAG
Yes, of course. Yes, well carry on
London.

                    GEORGE LONDON
As you know, sir, The Parkhurst
Observatory keeps a constant
surveillance on the alien spaceship
so it can monitor any change in its
position...

     *(Sir Lucas B. Windbag starts
     rustling some papers on his
     table and seems disinterested
     in George London's
     monologue.)*

...Last night, the alien spaceship
didn't just move, it exploded,
breaking into several thousand
pieces...

                  SIR LUCAS B. WINDBAG
Good lord, this is Friday, I'm
already late. Could you hurry this
up London, I've got to be somewhere.

     *(Sir Lucas B. Windbag is
     reading the name of a lady*

and an address written on his
book of matches.)

GEORGE LONDON
Most of the pieces, well, all but one
large chunk to be precise, burnt up
in the Earth's atmosphere.

SIR LUCAS B. WINDBAG
Yes, well that's a good thing isn't
it?

GEORGE LONDON
Yes it is, but unfortunately, the one
large chunk that didn't burn up was
over 300ft wide and crashed in the
Numenobman lake in Russia causing an
earthquake throughout the area.

SIR LUCAS B. WINDBAG
Good heavens, why wasn't I told about
this? This is the sort of thing MI5
should be investigating. Was anyone
injured? Did anyone die? Speak man,
speak!

GEORGE LONDON
Fortunately, it is a mountainous
region, many miles from the nearest
town and luckily nobody died. The
lake bore the brunt of the crash
along with the surrounding forest.

                    SIR LUCAS B. WINDBAG
Crashed in a lake, you say? Well,
this does complicate matters. There
could be valuable technology on that
ship, all sorts of space gizmos,
what?

                    GEORGE LONDON
Yes, sir.

                    SIR LUCAS B. WINDBAG
Well, I think we need to get there as
soon as possible, lord knows what
would happen to the balance of power
if France or Sweden got there
first...

        *(Sir Lucas B. Windbag takes a
        draw on his pipe.)*

...And of course, the Russians have a
head start on the lot of us. London,
here's what I want you to do for me.
Put together a small team of
mercenaries, use some of those ex-SAS
fellows, they like to throw
themselves out of a plane in the dead
of night. Get over to that crash
site and secure what you can. If you
are too late, and the Russians are
already there, I want you to blow it
up. Go and see Group Captain Tammy
T. Buckworthy at Oldham R.A.F base,
near Aldershot. Tell him, *'Binky
needs a new shoelace'* and he'll get

you what you need.

> GEORGE LONDON
> *'Binky needs a new shoelace'*, sir?

> SIR LUCAS B. WINDBAG
> Yes, that's it. Now trot along,
> there's a good fellow...

> (*George London looks at Sir
> Lucas B. Windbag
> quizzically.*)

> ...You're still here, was there
> something else, London?

> GEORGE LONDON
> It's nothing really, but, eh, how did
> you know the vicar was drinking a '54
> Beaujolais?

> SIR LUCAS B. WINDBAG
> Well it's obvious when you think
> about it. The pearls, London, the
> pearls. They were an absolute give
> away.

> GEORGE LONDON
> Yes of course, now you've explained
> it to me, it makes absolute sense.
> Yes, well cheerio sir.

                SIR LUCAS B. WINDBAG
Cheerio George, and good luck. Close
the door on your way out, there's a
good fellow.

    (George London leaves the
    room and closes the door.)

Scene fades.

ACT 2, SCENE 3

On the other side of the galaxy, on
planet EgÁs, a group of archaeologists
are camped out in the desert. Around
the encampment, hired workers hit the
ground with pickaxes and shovels.
Inside one of the tents, the leader of
the expedition, Sir Gorf Daot, and
five other archaeologists gather round
a wooden table. On the table, Sir
Daot points at a location on a map.
The group are all dressed in light tan
safari outfits and wear red cloth
hats. Except for their big head and
eyes and the absence of a little
finger, they look like Earthlings.
For the convenience of the reader, I
have translated their conversation
into English as The language of the
Dees-red-nÁ-Iroc people is very
difficult to read and sometimes
meaningless.

                 SIR GORF DAOT
I think we should be looking more in
this direction. If I'd wish to
conceal myself for thousands of
years, I would have gone deep into
these caves...

       (Sir Gorf Daot, a small fat
       fellow 4'7, points at the far
       Western corner of an area

known as, the Canyon of the
Kings.)

...I think we should start digging in
this area, just east of the camp...

*(Sir Gorf Daot takes out a
small thin white pipe and
stuffs it with a green leaf.)*

...Yes, if I was the leader of the
Great Council of Arkanazak, that's
where I would have my secret vault.
What do you think, Tac?

*(Tac, the tallest of the
group, points to a different
area on the map.)*

                    TAC
Well, I might be wrong, but I think
we ought to be looking more in this
direction, further south. An area
known as the *Valley of the Gods*. The
ancient scrolls of Arkanazak talk of
a jagged bluff and the mouth of a
Griff leading into a ribbon of water
that meets at the *Ra-eb's* Claw. As
you know, the *Griff* have been dead
for millennia, but records show that
it was a flightless bird with an
elongated beak. This region here, 3
miles south of us, has all of these
features...

(Tac runs his finger down the map.)

...Look here. A jagged bluff, leading into an elongated ridge - the Griff's beak. Then, a ribbon of water that splits into four separate channels and spills out down the east face of the cliff...

(Tac's hand moves across the map.)

...and finally, leading all the way to the Ra-eb's Claw. If you look closely at this section of the map, you can see the shape of three fingers and a thumb at the bottom of the rock face. This is where thousands of years of water erosion has eaten into the soft Emil stone.

(Sir Gorf Daot lights his pipe, takes a puff, then removes it from his mouth.)

SIR GORF DAOT
Mmm, you might be on to something there. Let me have a closer look...

(Sir Gorf Daot looks at the map and runs the mouth piece of his pipe along the ribbon of water.)

By Jove, I think you've cracked it
my boy. It was there all the time,
right under our noses. Wait until
the boys from the Ret-Se-crow club
hear about this.

                    TAC
Perhaps we should look in the area
first and see if I'm right.

                SIR GORF DAOT
Quite, yes. That's the thing to do.

        (Sir Gorf Daot walks outside
        the tent and shouts to the
        head worker to come over.)

                SIR GORF DAOT
Ah, Eeb, there you are. I don't want
to be a nuisance, but, well it's like
this ol' fellow...

        (Sir Gorf Daot puffs on his
        pipe.)

...We've been studying the old chart,
and I'm afraid we're going to have to
move camp ol' boy. I know we've only
just got set up here, but we've had a
bit of a break through...

        (Sir Gorf Daot puts his arm
        around Eeb.)

...So, if you could rally the men together and pass on the information.

(Eeb, *is a thin wiry chap from the ancient SelÁw tribe and is a geologist from the South-Western territories - he is in charge of the workers. He is dressed in a white robe and brown sandals. He looks at Sir Gorf Daot with annoyance.)*

                    EEB
I don't think the men are going to be very happy with you *boyo,* we've only just finished knocking in the last tent peg. The men are hungry and they need a rest...

(Eeb leans closer to Sir Daot.)

...What about we stay here for a couple of weeks, just poking the sand about a bit and shifting some stones from one area to another, and then tell the men we're moving on. That way, no one will feel that it was a waste of time erecting all this stuff, the men get a rest and you get to keep your credibility.

               SIR GROF DAOT
Credibility?

(Sir Gorf Daot puffs on his pipe and leans closer to Eeb.)

                    EEB
That's right, lost it is. This way
everyone is happy.

               SIR GORF DAOT
Well not everyone. I'll tell you
what we'll do Eeb. You and your men
can get something to eat, rest up and
get a good night's sleep. In the
morning, you and the men can pack
everything up and march south to the
Valley of the Gods.

                    EEB
Valley of the Gods you say. That's
at least 3 miles, we'll need three
days to get there.

               SIR GORF DAOT
Three days? Be set up by tomorrow
afternoon or find another job. Now,
go tell the men.

                    EEB
Yes, sir, right away.

Scene fades.

ACT 2, SCENE 4

Back on Earth, Yuri and Dmitry are still at the farmhouse. Inside the bedroom, they have found a wardrobe full of clothes and are searching through it for suitable attire.

                    YURI
What do you think of these?

        *(Yuri holds up a black pair
        of jeans, brown cowboy boots
        and a black T-shirt with a
        colourful image - a dog
        holding a ukulele.
        Underneath the image, the
        words read, 'My dog has
        fleas'.)*

                    DMITRY
Great...

        *(Dmitry finds a black leather
        jacket and holds it up to
        Yuri.)*

Perfect. Put this on, it will keep you warm on the motorbike.

                    YURI
Motorbike, aren't you forgetting something?

(*Dmitry holds up a blue shirt
across his chest.*)

DMITRY

What?

YURI

The motorbike has hole in petrol tank
and we have no petrol.

(*Dmitry pulls out some brown
trousers, work boots and a
grey sports jacket.*)

DMITRY

I have been thinking about that, and
I have a solution. Now, see if you
can find some socks in one of those
draws.

(*Yuri pulls open a brown
chest of drawers. Inside he
finds some socks and pants
and a leather pouch full of
money.*)

YURI

Dmitry, I have found some socks,
pants and some money.

DMITRY

Money?

(*Dmitry tries on the blue*

shirt.)

                    YURI
Yes, quite a bit.

                    DMITRY
Good. We will need some for food and
fuel. Take it, we will pay it back
later...

     *(Dmitry puts on the sports
     jacket.)*

...Besides, I think this place might
have belonged to that Popov guy, and
I don't think he'll be needing it.

                    YURI
What makes you think that?

     *(Dmitry points at a picture
     on the wall of Viktor Popov
     with an older man standing
     outside the farmhouse.)*

                    DMITRY
Now c'mon, get dressed. We're
getting out of here. The police
could come back at any moment to
search this place.

                    YURI
What about breakfast?

                    DMITRY
We will get something on way.

                     YURI
Breakfast is most important meal of
day.

                    DMITRY
Staying alive is more important than
your stomach. Now c'mon get moving.
I'll see you outside.

     *(Yuri finishes getting
     dressed and walks outside.
     Dmitry is pouring petrol from
     a jerry can into the petrol
     tank of the motorbike.)*

                     YURI
How did you fix tank?

                    DMITRY
I used clever trick I saw in old
black and white movie.

                     YURI
What was that?

                    DMITRY
The cork from whisky bottle. It is a
good fit for bullet hole.

                    YURI
And where did you get petrol from?

                    DMITRY
The police left jerry can behind
after they set fire to Citroen. It
was a quarter full. It should get us
a hundred miles down the road at
least.

                    YURI
Good. Where are we going?

                    DMITRY
I have a great aunt who lives 50
miles from here. We can hide there
for a couple of days and let heat die
down. It will also give us chance to
come up with plan.

                    YURI
Good. Hopefully we can find pie shop
on way.

Scene fades.

ACT 2, SCENE 5

Dmitry and Yuri have been travelling for 10 minutes on the motorbike. They are currently driving across a field and heading towards a gate that leads onto a back road.

                    DMITRY
Get off and open gate.

                    YURI
Okay, will do.

> *(Yuri dismounts from the motorbike and opens the gate. Dmitry drives onto the road and waits for Yuri. Up ahead on the road, an orange fiat 126 lies on its side. Yuri closes the gate and returns to the motorbike.)*

                    DMITRY
Look up there. A car is on its side. I think it is the car from the farmhouse.

> *(Yuri gets back on the bike.)*

                    YURI
Let's have a closer look...

(They drive up to the Fiat 126 and get off the bike.)

...Is there anyone inside.

(Dmitry looks inside the passenger window. A woman is lying dead on the front seat.)

                    DMITRY
Yes. It is the woman from the
farmhouse. She is dead.

                    YURI
How did she crash, I can't see
anything she could have hit.

                    DMITRY
She was shot.

                    YURI
Shot? How do you know that?

                    DMITRY
There is a bullet hole through the
windscreen and her face is full of
blood.

     (Yuri looks on agitated.)

                    YURI
Dmitry, let's get out of here.

(Dmitry walks back to the
motorbike. Yuri gets on the
back and they leave. They
travel another 200 yards and
come upon a UAZ-452 military
police vehicle parked in the
middle of the road. Its
doors are open and blood
covers the vehicle. Four
policemen lay dead in various
locations on the road.
Behind the steering wheel,
LT. Tapovich lies slumped
over on the seat, he is
moaning. Dmitry stops and
looks.)

YURI
What is going on Dmitry?

DMITRY
I don't know, Popov and Ivanov must
have escaped. Look, someone is
moving.

(Dmitry gets off the
motorbike.)

YURI
Where are you going?

DMITRY
To see if I can help.

                    YURI
We should leave Dmitry.

          (Dmitry walks up to the
          police vehicle and pulls LT.
          Tapovich up from his slumped
          position.)

                    DMITRY
What happened here?

                  LT. TAPOVICH
I've been shot, call an ambulance.

                    DMITRY
In a minute. Who shot you?

                  LT. TAPOVICH
I am injured, get me some help.

          (Dmitry looks down at the
          wound in the lieutenant's
          stomach.)

                    DMITRY
It is too late for that. Now, tell
me what is going on.

                  LT. TAPOVICH
Who are you?

                    DMITRY
Don't worry about that, just tell me

who shot you. Was it Viktor Popov?

*(The lieutenant moans and
grabs Dmitry's arm.)*

                    LT. TAPOVICH
No, it was the army, General
Gerasimov's men. He was not here,
but his men were. They all had the
Special Forces tattoo pertaining to
his platoon - two leaves of Romaine
lettuce with an anchovy swimming in
the centre. Underneath the emblem,
the Latin words highlight their
motto: 'IGITUR QUI DESIDERAT PISCIS,
PRAEPARET ACETARIA'.

                    DMITRY
'If you want fish, prepare for
salad'.

                    LT. TAPOVICH
Yes, that's it. You know your
Latin...

*(LT. Tapovich moves his
position and pulls himself
forward by grabbing the
steering wheel. He coughs
for a moment, then looks up
at Dmitry. He waves his
right index finger into the
air and begins to speak
again.)*

...They came out of the trees, just like monkeys. Before we knew what had happened, it was over. They took Popov and Ivanov and killed everyone else.

                    DMITRY
What do they want with them, why didn't they just kill them?

        (Lt. Tapovich grips Dmitry's
        arm. Yuri looks up and down
        the road impatiently puffing
        on a cigarette.)

                LT. TAPOVICH
Get me help?

                    DMITRY
Alright, I will get help, but first answer my questions. Why did they take Popov and Ivanov?

                LT. TAPOVICH
I don't know. They said something about the two dead Russian cosmonauts Dmitry Usakov and Yuri Chekov. The head guy, a man dressed in black, spoke to somebody on the radio and said they had secured the package and were heading back to base. I believe one of the soldiers referred to him as Vadim, but I can't be sure. I thought he was odd looking at first,

until I noticed he had...

> *(The lieutenant moans and*
> *passes out.)*

                    YURI
What is happening Dmitry, what is he
saying?

                    DMITRY
Just wait a minute. Keep a look out.

> *(Dmitry turns back to the*
> *lieutenant and shakes him.)*

                    DMITRY
Wake up! Wake up you stupid cop...

> *(The lieutenant starts to*
> *come round.)*

...What did you notice about the man
in black?

                 LT. TAPOVICH
His face was severely burned and he
only had three fingers on his left
hand...

> *(The lieutenant starts to*
> *cough.)*

You're Dmitry Usakov, I thought I
recognised you. You are alive.

How?... How can this be?...

> *(The lieutenant dies and falls against the steering wheel. The car horn erupts into life and Dmitry pulls him away from the wheel and the sound stops.)*

                    YURI
C'mon, what is taking so long. Let's get out of here.

                    DMITRY
I'm coming. He can't help us any more, he's dead.

> *(Dmitry and Yuri return to the motorbike and drive off.)*

Scene fades.

ACT 2. SCENE 6

Friday 17th October, 9.12am. George London and a group of ex-SAS soldiers arrive at Oldham R.A.F airbase in a Bedford MK truck. At the gates, they are given directions to aircraft hanger 21 in the far west corner. They drive for two minutes, park outside the hanger and wait for Captain T. Buckworthy to arrive. Shortly afterwards, The captain arrives in an Austin Champ Jeep. George London exits his truck and goes to meet the captain.

GEORGE LONDON
Are you Captain Buckworthy?

(The captain walks over to meet George London. Buckworthy is in his late 50's and walks with a stick. He is thin, and sports a natural moustache.)

CAPT. T. BUCKWORHTY
Please, call me Tammy...

(They shake hands.)

...Now, what can I do for you?

                    GEORGE LONDON
I need some equipment and an aircraft
to take us to Russia.

                  CAPT. T. BUCKWORTHY
Equipment and an aircraft, that's
different. What sort of equipment?

                    GEORGE LONDON
The usual - hand guns, rifles,
knives, radios, binoculars, grenades,
explosives, bullets that sort of
thing...

          (George London pulls out a
          comprehensive list from his
          pocket and looks at it.)

...Oh, and parachutes. Bit of a pest
jumping out of a plane without one,
always seem to break a leg...

          (He hands the list over to
          Captain T. Buckworthy.)

...Mind you, always seem to get hung
up in a tree when I've got one of the
blasted things, but I suppose it's
better than a snapped tibia, what?

                  CAPT. T. BUCKWORTHY
Oh, I see. It's a bit unusual.
Don't usually give this sort of stuff
away, it's more in the line of caps

and badges...

    (Buckworthy looks at the
    list.)

...Did give away a gas mask once for
the boy scouts summer raffle, but
even that had some damage.

    (Buckworthy folds up the list
    and hands it back to George
    London.)

...Sorry, can't help you I'm afraid.
Never give this sort of stuff away,
especially when it's for the local
jumble sale to raise money for
Christmas tree lights...

    (Buckworthy starts to walk
    away. London follows.)

...Waste of time, if you ask me.

          GEORGE LONDON
I have nothing to do with a jumble
sale. I was told if I came to see
you, you could supply us with these
things?

    (Buckworthy looks at London.)

                    CAPT. T. BUCKWORTHY
Who by?

                      GEORGE LONDON
The head of MI5, Sir Lucas B.
Windbag.

                    CAPT. T. BUCKWORTHY
Old Windbag, is he still head of MI5?
Well I never. Still can't help you
I'm afraid.

                      GEORGE LONDON
But this is of the utmost
importance...

        (George London looks down at
        his list. On the bottom of
        the paper the words, 'Binky
        has a new shoelace'. He
        shouts them out.)

...Binky has a new shoelace.

        (Capt. T. Buckworthy stops in
        his tracks, turns around and
        walks back to George London.)

                    CAPT. T. BUCKWORTHY
Why the devil didn't you say so in
the first place. Come with me, I'll
get you everything you need for your
trip...

(Capt. T. Buckworthy starts to walk to the back of the hanger.)

...Got some really good stuff in this next room. All the latest gadgets for a fun filled holiday abroad.

Scene fades.

ACT 2. SCENE 7

Friday 17th October, 9.56am. Yuri and Dmitry have been riding their motorbike for over an hour and are getting close to Dmitry's great aunt's house. Up ahead, a small village by the name of Vlogomvich is holding their annual Mooncalf festival. Children dressed as goats, birds, fish, monkeys, gold coins, treasure chests, bananas, pork pies, lemons and triangles of blue cheese walk down the pavement with their mothers in tow. Wagons carrying people dressed as tarot cards, bulls, ravens, jesters and snakes, roll down the streets being pulled by unicorns. Tambourines, whistles, bells, harps and drums fill the air like wind caught in a drain pipe.

                    YURI
What is going on here?

        (Dmitry slows down and looks
        for a way through the busy
        streets.)

                    DMITRY
Don't know. Must be some sort of carnival.

                    YURI
Looks pretty scary. Children dressed
as blue cheese and goats is a
disturbing sight...

     *(Yuri looks around and sees a
     newsagent.)*

...Pull over there, there is a
newsagent. I want to get cigarettes.

     *(Dmitry pulls over to the
     side of the road.)*

                  DMITRY
Yuri, get me a little something to
warm me up.

                    YURI
Okay, I'll see you in a minute.

     *(Dmitry walks inside the
     newsagent and goes up to the
     counter. He is greeted by a
     man wearing a seahorse
     costume.)*

                SEAHORSE MAN
What can I get you?

                    YURI
Could I get two packets of Karlburo
and a litre bottle of whisky.

SEAHORSE MAN

What brand?

(Yuri points to a bottle. In the shop he glances at crystals, wands, amulets, sun dials, silver jewellery and various masks.)

YURI

The single malt there, the Glengrenfear.

(The seahorse man hands over the items.)

SEAHORSE MAN

Anything else?

YURI

Eh, yes. I'll take that frog mask and the...

(Yuri looks at the various masks on display.)

...And the bear one.

(The Seahorse man hands them over. He then rings everything up on the till.)

                    SEAHORSE MAN
That'll be 4000 Rubles please.

          (Yuri puts his hand in his
          pocket to get the money.)

                       YURI
Looks like you're having a festival
here today?

                  SEAHORSE MAN
Yes, it's the town's annual Mooncalf
carnival. This year we celebrate its
423rd year...

          (The Seahorse man opens the
          till.)

...Didn't think we would have it this
year after last night's storm, but
everything's bright and clear this
morning - must have the luck of the
gods on our side for a change...

          (Yuri counts out the money
          and the Seahorse man looks
          out the window at the
          parade.)

...This morning, we will dance around
and sing songs, play games, drink
beer and feast on sous-vide carrots
and parsnips. In the afternoon we
will pay special tribute to the
town's founder, Yagor Pyritevich by

marching to the old family farm and
search for his lost gold.

                    YURI
Lost gold, how did he lose it?

                 SEAHORSE MAN
He didn't. He died suddenly and
nobody knew where he hid his fortune.
Over the years, the family searched
for it, but were unsuccessful. Now,
it's no more than a legend, but the
town's folk have adopted it as their
own and feel it's their right to keep
the search going. So, once a year,
the good people of Vlogomvich march
up to the old family farm of
Pyritevich and walk in the fields
with metal detectors searching for
the gold...

     (The Seahorse man points to
     the corner of the shop.)

...There are treasure maps over there
if you want one and shovels by the
door.

                    YURI
No thanks, maybe another time. Here,
keep the change.

     (The man looks down at the
     money.)

                    SEAHORSE MAN
Thanks very much.

>   (Outside the shop, Yuri trips
>   over a man dressed as a
>   crescent moon and falls to
>   the ground scraping his
>   forearm.

                     MOON MAN
Why don't you watch where you're
going, nearly damaged one of my
stars. You ought to be more careful.
Don't you know there's a carnival
going on?...

>   (The Moon Man continues to
>   walk on.)

...Some people have got no sense of
propriety when they see a moon
walking by.

>   (Yuri gets up to confront the
>   Moon Man but stops suddenly
>   when he sees two military
>   policemen and four armed
>   soldiers walking down the
>   street. The policemen and
>   the soldiers seem to be
>   searching for someone and are
>   showing photos to the crowd.
>   Yuri puts on the frog mask
>   and walks back over to
>   Dmitry.)

                    YURI
Dmitry, put this on. There are real
gremlins in the crowd.

        (Dmitry looks up the street
        and sees the police and the
        army. He puts on his bear
        mask.)

                    DMITRY
I'll take this back street, I think
we can get to my great aunt's farm
this way.

                    YURI
How much further?

                    DMITRY
Only about one mile.

                    YURI
Good.

Scene fades.

ACT 2. SCENE 8

The following day On EgÁs, The sun glows hot in a lemon yellow sky. In the Valley of the Gods, the afternoon heat bakes the golden sand to a cool 70°C and the red rocks and outcrops scattered on the valley floor become unbearable to the touch. Sir Gorf Daot and his expedition are nearing the end of their journey and have had an arduous three mile trek to Ra-eb's Claw. Most of the men are exhausted and are suffering from dehydration. Under the intolerable furnace, Tac stops for a while in the shade and lets the men walk past. In his hands, he holds a map of the region and studies it for a while. He starts to give instructions to the men for making camp, then stops to look at someone.

                    TAC
You there?

          (A small thin man with a dark
          tan is putting some sun block
          on his nose. He is at the
          end of a long line of men
          carrying equipment.)

                    DARK TAN MAN
Who me?

                    TAC
Yes, you...

        (Tac points at the man.)

...Where's your equipment?

                    DARK TAN MAN
Equipment?

                    TAC
Yes, equipment?

                    DARK TAN MAN
I've lost it.

                    TAC
What do you mean you've lost it?

                    DARK TAN MAN
Well, I know where it is, I just
don't have it with me right now.

        (Tac walks over to the man.)

                    TAC
Look here, every man in this
expedition was supplied with a kit.
I simply want to know where yours is?

                    DARK TAN MAN
Well, seeing as you are pushing the
point. I left it at the bottom of
Cobblers Toe near *Yak* ravine.

                      TAC
That was nearly 7 days ago. What
have you been using for a shovel?

                    DARK TAN MAN
Well, I didn't get rid of all my
equipment. I kept the mess kit and
I've been digging with a frying pan.

        *(Tac looks for Eeb in the
        line of men and shouts out to
        him.)*

                      TAC
Eeb, where are you man? Come here at
once.

        *(At the front of the line,
        Eeb's head pops out and he
        starts to walk back towards
        Tac.)*

                      EEB
Yes, sir, what is it?

                      TAC
This man...

        (Tac points at the dark tan

man.)

...This man, has been without his
equipment for the last seven days.
He has just informed me he left it at
Cobbler's Toe. Did you know this?

                    EEB
Yes, I did, sir.

                    TAC
You did. Well...

     *(Tac looks upset and is
     momentarily at a loss for
     words.)*

...What have you got to say for
yourself?

                    EEB
He's not alone.

                    TAC
He's not alone, what does that mean?

                    EEB
It means some of the other men left
their stuff at *Cobblers Toe* as well.

     (Tac paces back and forth.)

TAC

This is an outrage. Wait until Sir Daot hears about this. Dear, oh dear...

(Tac continues to pace.)

...Why did they leave their stuff behind. C'mon Eeb answer me. This is your responsibility y'know, you're suppose to monitor the men's behaviour and keep them in check. I don't mind the odd liberty and the poking fun at Sir Daot, but this is scandalous; men leaving equipment behind, whatever next? Suppose we all left valuable supplies behind: tents, food, water - the compass; where would we be then?...

(Tac takes a moment to calm down, and then begins again.)

...It all costs money y'know, if it wasn't for the funding supplied to us by the women's crochet club, we couldn't even afford to have this expedition. Women like them work tirelessly joining bits of yarn together to make blankets for the cold and impoverished, not to mention the colourful baby bobble hats they produce for the starving children of OnÁgero Defnu. If it wasn't for the support of these types of groups, we couldn't even afford a shovel...

>   *(Tac looks at the dark tanned*
>   *man.)*

...And you leave it behind. I've got
a good mind to thrash the lot of you
and put you on half rations. Now, I
want answers.

                    EEB
Well, it's like this boyo. The men
were getting a bit tired of moving
camp everyday and walking in the
baking hot sun with all that stuff,
so they left it behind. Anyway,
Nelson here...

>   *(Eeb points at the dark*
>   *tanned man.)*

...By-the-way, this is Nelson.
Nelson noticed we were walking in a
big circle, and suggested to the men
that they leave most of their
equipment behind because they would
only be walking back to it in a few
days time...

>   *(Nelson is nodding at Tac.)*

...Of course, not all of the men
listened to him, 'cause they didn't
want to get into any trouble. But as
you can see...

(*Eeb points at the* Cobbler's Toe *section of the rock face.*)

...He was right.

(*Tac takes out a small tin from his pocket, removes a pink pill and puts it in his mouth. He looks agitated and his left eye is twitching.*)

                    TAC
What do you mean he was right?
Nelson just told me he left his
equipment at '*Cobbler's Toe*' seven
days ago. We are now in the Valley
of the Gods at Ra-eb's Claw.

(*Eeb looks at the map Tac is holding.*)

                    EEB
Can I see your map, sir?

                    TAC
Yes, of course, but be careful, it's
actually Sir Daot's. You'll soon see
who's right.

                    EEB
Right, I see what's happened...

(Eeb shows the map to Tac.)

...This map is over 50 years old.
They renamed *Ra-eb's Claw* 47 years
ago to *Cobbler's Toe*.

                    TAC
What?

                    EEB
They renamed it.

                    TAC
Why would they do that?

                    EEB
Well, I am surprised. Imagine you
not knowing the story of the
Cobbler's Toe. I would have thought
with you being an archaeologist and a
man into all that history stuff, you
would have known. Well I never.

                    TAC
Known what? Look here Eeb, tell me
what's going on?

                    EEB
We're back at Cobbler's Toe.
Otherwise known as Ra-eb's Claw.

                    NELSON
He's right boyo. If you don't

believe us, just look over the other
side of that rock and you'll see all
our equipment from seven days ago.

> (Tac walks over to the rock
> and sees the equipment. Sir
> Gorf Daot walks into the
> scene.)

                SIR GORF DAOT
Ah, Tac, there you are. Everything
alright?

> (Tac looks a bit embarrassed
> and confused.)

                TAC
Yes, sir, everything's fine. I was
just telling the men where to set up
camp.

                SIR GORF DAOT
Jolly good. I was just looking up at
that long ridge up there...

> (Sir Gorf Daot points at the
> cliff top.)

...looks frightfully familiar, just
like that other place we were at a
few days ago, what was it called -
The Gobbler's Mouth or something.
Then again, the desert does look the
same everywhere you go, all that

sand, what?...

> *(Sir Gorf Daot starts to walk*
> *away and then turns around.)*

...Oh, you haven't seen my map
anywhere have you?

> *(Tac hands him his map.)*

                    TAC
There you are, sir.

                SIR GORF DAOT
Oh, excellent. It's a bit tatty, but
dear old aunt Agatha gave it to me.
Perhaps I'll get a new one, one of
these days...

> *(Sir Gorf Daot walks away and*
> *waves the map in the air.)*

...It'll save me borrowing your one
all the time, what?

> *(Tac turns back to face Eeb.)*

                    TAC
Yes, well, let's not say anything
further on the matter. Eeb, if you
tell the men to set up camp over
there. After they have finished,
they can relax for the rest of the
day. We will start digging first

thing tomorrow at the bottom of that
ridge over there.

                    EEB
Very good, sir.

        (*Tac walks away from the men
        and then turns back.*)

                    TAC
Oh, Eeb? We haven't been digging in
that area already have we?

                    EEB
No. The last time we were here, we
only stayed for 3 hours and then we
moved onto the *Gaping Jaw*, in the
valley of the slaves.

                    TAC
Yes, that's right, I remember now.
Yes, well, carry on.

Scene fades.

ACT 2. SCENE 9

Friday 17th October, 10.24am, one mile outside the village of Vlogomvich. Dmitry and Yuri turn up an old dirt track that leads through a woodland. Up ahead of them is an old farmhouse and some odd looking garden ornaments. In the courtyard, geese, ducks and chickens roam around scratching for food. Three big barrage balloons, anchored to the ground by cables, sway gently above the house. In the garden, a big telescope peers out of the top of a white, orb-shaped observatory. As They approach the farmhouse, they stop, get off their motorbike, cover it with fir tree branches and start to walk into the garden. As they near the house gate, a woman appears dressed in an orange Hazmat suit holding a shotgun.

                    HAZMAT WOMAN
Hold it right there!

          (The woman points the shotgun
          at Yuri and Dmitry. She has
          a rustic American accent
          mixed with Russian. Her
          inflection is peculiar to the
          area and you can just hear a
          slight Irish lilt at the end
          of her sentence. Under her

hazmat helmet it is difficult to pinpoint the woman's exact origins as the voice may be distorted due to the face mask. Dmitry and Yuri stand motionless.)

DMITRY

Yuri, don't move. I will handle this.

(Dmitry walks towards the woman and she shoots a metal wind chime that hangs next to them.)

HAZMAT WOMAN

I told you fellows not to move. What do you want here?...

(The Hazmat woman walks closer to them.)

...You...

(She points at Yuri with the shotgun.)

...You with the frog face, why are you here?

YURI

We are looking for my friend's great aunt.

                    HAZMAT WOMAN
Why, is she lost?

                        YURI
No, I believe she lives here.

                    HAZMAT WOMAN
Is this your friend, this funny
looking fella with the facial hair?

                        YURI
Yes.

                    HAZMAT WOMAN
What's your friends name?

                        YURI
Dmitry, Dmitry Usakov.

                    HAZMAT WOMAN
Dmitry Usakov? He's dead. Saw it on
the news myself. Got himself blowed
up in the *Space Station* with that
other fella Yuri something.

                        DMITRY
Great aunt Charlotte. Is that you?
It's me Dmitry.

                    HAZMAT WOMAN
Nobody calls me that, not any more.
Everyone I ever knew is dead.

*(She lowers the gun slightly,
then raises it again.)*

HAZMAT WOMAN
Ah, this is a deceitful trick, I must
be having one of my turns. If you're
Dmitry Usakov, what did you call me
as a boy?

*(Dmitry pulls his bear mask
off.)*

DMITRY
Well, as a child, I couldn't say
great aunt charlotte, I used to say,
'gate ant haslet'. From then
onwards, I just called you Hazzie.

HAZZIE
Dmitry, it really is you...

*(She lowers her gun and
removes her helmet.)*

...How is this possible?

(Yuri removes his frog mask.)

DMITRY
If you make us some of that fine
Sweet Cicely tea you used to make me
as a child, I will tell you all about
our woeful exploits.

                    HAZZIE
Sure, I think I have some fresh
plants out back.

        (Hazzie, Dmitry and Yuri
        enter the house. In the
        kitchen, Dmitry and Yuri sit
        at an old oak table while
        Hazzie wanders off in the
        back garden to get some Sweet
        Cicely for the tea. The
        kitchen is nicely rustic with
        hanging pans and lanterns,
        but on closer inspection, it
        reveals twisted metal shapes,
        sharp metallic objects and
        miniature gyroscopes. Layers
        of dust cover most of the
        items on display giving them
        a sepia tone.)

                    YURI
A nice place your great aunt has
here.

                    DMITRY
You should have seen it when great
uncle Yakov was alive. What a
character, always inventing
something...

        (Dmitry looks around.)

...He had a car that ran on ring
pulls from soda cans and a bicycle

with square wheels.

                    YURI
Ring pulls? Sounds impossible.

                  DMITRY
That's what I thought, but I saw it
with my own eyes.

                    YURI
So, what happened to it?

                  DMITRY
Just as he was about to market the
idea, the soda companies changed the
design of the pull mechanism on the
can and there was no more ring pulls.
Almost overnight the gutters and
pavements were clear.

                    YURI
I remember, it was a terrible
problem, they were everywhere; that
and cigarette packets - what a mess.

                  DMITRY
My uncle was convinced that the oil
industry persuaded the soda companies
to change the design of the can to
stop the inevitable downfall of its
worth and use.

     (From outside the back

garden, Hazzie returns with
some Sweet Cicely and a slice
of honey comb.)

HAZZIE
I'm back. Took longer than I
thought. I've got some hemlock at
the bottom of the garden and I didn't
want to get the wrong plant and kill
us all.

DMITRY
No, that would have been a tragedy.

HAZZIE
It won't be long now. Just got to
wait for the kettle to boil...

   (Hazzie turns around to face
   them.)

...What have you boys been talking
about?

YURI
Dmitry was telling me about your late
husband's invention - the ring pull
car.

HAZZIE
Yes, he is late isn't he. He should
have been home hours ago, I only sent
him out for the paper.

                    YURI
But I thought your husband was dead?

                   HAZZIE
Yakov? No, who told you that?

                    YURI
Dmitry did, I think. Didn't you
Dmitry?

     *(The kettle starts to
     whistle.)*

                   HAZZIE
That's the kettle. I'll make the
tea.

     *(Yuri looks at Dmitry and
     whispers to him.)*

                    YURI
Dmitry, is he dead?

     *(Dmitry looks at Yuri and
     whispers back to him.)*

                   DMITRY
I hope so, we buried him 15 years
ago.

     (Hazzie turns back around.)

                    HAZZIE
There we are. You boys help yourself
to that and I'll see if I've got some
biscuits.

          *(Hazzie leaves the kitchen to
          go to the pantry.)*

                    YURI
Dmitry, is she alright?

                    DMITRY
She was always a little eccentric,
but I think maybe the wheel has
slipped from the wagon.

                    YURI
Shh, she is coming back.

          *(Hazzie returns empty
          handed.)*

                    HAZZIE
You boys are back early, did you have
a good day at school?

          (Dmitry looks at Yuri.)

                    DMITRY
Yes, not bad.

                    HAZZIE
Good. You haven't touched your tea,

let me pour it for you.

    (Hazzie pours the tea. Yuri
    tastes it.)

             YURI
Mmm, this tea is delicious. What a
nice taste of aniseed and liquorice,
and that fresh honey - what a treat.

           HAZZIE
I'm glad you like it Yegor.

    (Yuri looks at Dmitry.)

           DMITRY
Hazzie, do you have a phone? I wish
to make a call.

           HAZZIE
Yes, there is one in the hall.

           DMITRY
Thank you, I won't be a minute.

    (Yuri pulls Dmitry's arm.)

           YURI
Who are you calling?

           DMITRY
Everything is a lot more complicated
than we thought, we are in real

trouble. I feel the net closing in. If we don't let somebody know we are alive, there is nothing stopping them from killing us. I am going to phone an old friend of mine who works for the *Space Programme*, I have known him a long time and he will know what to do. Once I speak to him, he will contact the relevant people and our troubles will be over.

                    YURI
That is good news.

        *(Dmitry leaves the room to go
        and use the phone.)*

                  HAZZIE
You must be hungry after your sack race, would you like some soup?

        *(Yuri looks at Hazzie
        confused.)*

                    YURI
What kind is it.

                  HAZZIE
Chicken and vegetable, made it fresh this morning. Just have to heat it up.

                    YURI
Chicken and vegetable, yes please.

(Hazzie turns on the stove to heat up the soup. Then turns to face Yuri again.)

HAZZIE

It's real nice having you here, but where did your lady friend go to?

(Yuri looks at her perplexed.)

YURI

Lady friend? Oh, he, I mean she, she went to use the phone.

HAZZIE

Don't you just love the daffodils in spring time, so yellow. Do you like flowers?

(Hazzie points to a window box with dead flowers and weeds.)

YURI

Yes, they are very pretty.

(Dmitry returns from using the phone.)

HAZZIE

Dmitry, what are you doing here, they said you were dead?

                    DMITRY
Yes, well, you can't believe
everything you read in the Paper.

        (Hazzie goes to the cupboard
        to get some soup bowls and
        then places them on the
        table. She leaves the room
        and walks into the hall.)

                    YURI
Dmitry, your great aunt is a little
loopy.

                    DMITRY
Yes, it would appear her health has
deteriorated since my last visit.

                    YURI
How did you get on with your phone
call, is your friend going to help
us?

        (Dmitry looks a little
        forlorn.)

                    DMITRY
It would seem the world is against us
Yuri.

                    YURI
What do you mean?

DMITRY

The phone didn't work. At first I
thought maybe the wire was unplugged,
but when I picked up phone to check
the back, it was as light as a
feather. Someone has removed the
innards and filled it with Ring
Pulls.

YURI

I am guessing that someone was your
great uncle Yakov.

(Hazzie returns from the
hall.)

HAZZIE

I'll get your soup and then you can
go out and play...

(Hazzie dishes out the soup.)

HAZZIE

...Oh, I've forgotten the thyme.
Must have a fresh bit of thyme. You
boys go ahead and eat, and I'll go
and cut some.

(Hazzie walks out into the
garden. Yuri tries the
soup.)

                    YURI
What an unusual tasting soup,
terrible after taste of cheese and
soap...

        (Yuri puts his spoon down.)

...Dmitry, go and see what is in soup
pan.

        *(Dmitry gets up and goes over
        to the bubbling cauldron on
        the stove. He lifts the lid
        and looks in.)*

                    DMITRY
It is chicken and vegetable soup, but
it also appears that she is washing
her socks and underwear in here as
well. If I was you, I wouldn't...

        *(Dmitry turns around holding
        a sock on the end of a spoon.
        Yuri is nowhere to been
        seen.)*

...Eat anymore.

        *(Dmitry wanders out into the
        garden. Outside he sees Yuri
        being sick. He goes over to
        him. Yuri stands up and
        wipes his mouth.)*

                    YURI
Y'know Dmitry, I sometimes wish that
man on train had been a librarian or
a mattress tester.

          (Dmitry pats Yuri on the
          shoulder.)

                   DMITRY
What? Look at all the fun you would
have missed.

          (Dmitry looks around the
          garden. The grass is
          overgrown and the weeds are
          high. A moon dial peeps up
          above a group of proud
          nettles; its face is old and
          worn. At the back of the
          garden a huge greenhouse made
          out of plastic bottles and
          soda cans casts a shadow on
          the lawn. The vegetable
          patch is overgrown and a
          rusty garden fork handle
          spies through a clump of
          broad-leaved docks.)

                    YURI
Dmitry, I am tired. Let's go back
inside and get a rest for a while.

                    DMITRY
Okay. What a shame, used to be
lovely here.

        (*Hazzie returns from the
        bottom of the garden holding
        some thyme.*)

                    HAZZIE
Thyme's not growing so well this
year, been a bit dry. Come back
inside and I'll get you some more
soup.

Scene fades.

ACT 2. SCENE 10

Friday 17th October, 11.03am. In the town of Vlogomvich, the town's people are making merry and eating their carrots and parsnips by the truck load. The military police and soldiers are still on the streets questioning the public and showing photos of Yuri and Dmitry. One policeman walks into the newsagent and questions the man dressed as a seahorse.

                    POLICEMAN
Excuse me, but have you seen these men?

          *(The policeman holds up
          Dmitry and Yuri's picture.)*

                    SEAHORSE MAN
No, I don't think so...

          *(The Seahorse man looks at
          Yuri's picture closer and
          points at it.)*

...No wait, this one was in here earlier.

                    POLICEMAN
At what time exactly?

                    SEAHORSE MAN
Maybe 40 minutes ago. Why, what have
they done?

                    POLICEMAN
They are just needed for questioning,
that's all. Did you happen to see
which way they went?

                    SEAHORSE MAN
No, sorry, the street was too busy,
but I did see him walk over to
another guy on a motorbike.

                    POLICEMAN
Well, thank you for your help.

        (The policeman walks out of
        the newsagent and is tripped
        up by a man wearing a
        crescent moon. He falls to
        the ground and scrapes his
        forearm.)

                    MOON MAN
Why don't you watch where you're
going, nearly damaged one of my
stars. You ought to be more careful.
Don't you know there's a carnival
going on?...

        (The policeman gets back to
        his feet.)

...Some people have got no sense of propriety when they see a moon walking by.

> (The policeman calls out to one of the soldiers.)

POLICEMAN
Sergeant? Arrest this man.

SERGEANT
Yes, sir.

> (The sergeant grabs the Moon Man by the arm and marches him off to the police wagon.)

MOON MAN
Wait a minute, I was only having a laugh. Can't you take a joke?

> (The policeman waves to the soldiers to come back to the van. When they are gathered together he speaks.)

POLICEMAN
The two fugitives we've been looking for were spotted here about 40 minutes ago, so they must be close. We will keep looking for another 2 hours and then we'll move on. Everyone meet back here at precisely 1.10pm.

*(The policeman addresses the
sergeant.)*

POLICEMAN

That moon guy in the van keeps making
silly, stupid expressions. He is
annoying me. Go and punch him in the
face.

SERGEANT

Yes, sir. I'll go and do that right
now...

*(The sergeant walks away and
then looks back.)*

...How hard, sir?

POLICEMAN

What?

SERGEANT

How hard would you like me to punch
him in the face.

POLICEMAN

Are there different levels of
hardness?

SERGEANT

Oh, yes. They range from a gentle
slap, which will just leave a red
mark on his face for half an hour, to

a hard punch that will knock his
teeth out and likely give him brain
damage.

> (The Moon Man in the van is
> listening to the conversation
> between the policeman and the
> sergeant and his face has
> changed from that of an
> annoying jester to a scared
> rabbit. The policeman looks
> up at the Moon Man whilst
> rubbing his sore arm.)

POLICEMAN

Hmm. I think maybe a gentle slap to
start with and if his attitude
doesn't change you can beat him to
death.

SERGEANT

Right, consider it done.

> (The sergeant enters the van
> and slaps the Moon Man in the
> face.)

MOON MAN

Now look what you've done, you've
broken my moon. That took my aunt
two weeks to make that - cracked
right down the middle, you've ruined
it; all the sequins are comin' off.
I'll never get first prize for best

original outfit in the over 30's
now...

(The Moon Man looks up at the
sergeant.)

...Well I hope you're happy, you big
brute. I don't know what my mother's
going to say?

(The sergeant walks back
outside to the policeman.)

                POLICEMAN
Keep him quiet, we don't want to
attract any unnecessary attention.
I'm going to look around, stay here
and watch him.

                SERGEANT
Okay.

(The Moon Man leans forward
on the seat and shouts out.)

                MOON MAN
I've seen who you are looking for!

(The policeman stops walking
and goes back to the wagon.)

                POLICEMAN
What did you say?

                    MOONMAN
I've seen who you are looking for.
They were here about 45 minutes ago.

                    POLICEMAN
Go on?

                    MOON MAN
Will you let me go if I tell you?

        (The policeman looks at the
        sergeant and then back at the
        Moon Man.)

                    POLICEMAN
If you cooperate and tell us what you
know, yes, I will...

        (The policeman shows the Moon
        Man pictures of Dmitry and
        Yuri.)

...Was this who you saw?

                    MOON MAN
Yes. This one...

        (The Moon Man points at
        Yuri.)

...He was in the shop buying
cigarettes and whisky. He also
bought a frog mask and a bear mask.
After I tripped, I mean, he fell

over, he put on the frog mask and
walked over to a man on a motorcycle.
He handed the other man the bear
mask. He put it on and they left.

                    POLICEMAN
Which way did they go?

                    MOON MAN
They went up that road there, that's
all I know...

     (The Moon Man reaches into a
     purse and pulls out a
     handkerchief and wipes his
     eyes.)

...Now, can I go?

                    POLICEMAN
No. Keep him there sergeant.

     (The policeman goes outside
     and blows a whistle. Moments
     later, soldiers begin to
     return to the wagon.)

                    MOON MAN
Oh, you varlet. I'll never trust a
man in uniform again.

Scene fades.

ACT 2. SCENE 11

12.43pm. At Hazzie's farmhouse, Yuri and Dmitry have been asleep for 2 hours in a spare bedroom. Downstairs, Hazzie has been busy in the kitchen cooking pies, sausage rolls, lasagne, savoury rice, boiled eggs and a baked whole salmon. Lemon tarts, pastries and cakes sit on a display carousel and the house smells fantastic. As a fine breeze wafts into the house through an open kitchen window, the aroma of cooking winds its way up the stairs and finds its way to Yuri's olfactory system; he wakes up.

                    YURI
Dmitry, are you are awake?

                    DMITRY
No.

                    YURI
I think we better get up.

                    DMITRY
Why? Whenever we are awake, we are running for our lives. Besides my head is splitting.

                    YURI
That's because you drink too much.

                    DMITRY
My head hurts because it needs a top
up. What did you do with whisky?

                     YURI
It is in the saddle bag on motorbike
along with my cigarettes...

    (Yuri sits up.)

...If you get up, I will go and get
it, but we must find something to
eat, I am feeling weak.

                    DMITRY
Okay, I will get up. See if any of
those chickens outside have laid an
egg.

                     YURI
That is worth a shot. I will see you
in a minute.

    (Yuri gets dressed then walks
    outside to get the whisky and
    cigarettes. On his way back
    to the farmhouse, he looks in
    the barn for eggs. Inside,
    there are hundreds of boxes
    stacked to the ceiling. The
    roof is damaged and you can
    see the sky. On the floor, a
    soggy box spills out its
    contents from one corner to

*reveal thousands of soda can
ring pulls. He looks among
the boxes for a while to find
eggs, but the floorboards
seems spongy and unsafe so he
returns to the farmhouse.
Inside, Dmitry is watching a
T.V. in the living room and
drinking some tea. Yuri
walks into the room to join
him.)*

DMITRY
Did you get any eggs?

YURI
No, but here is your whisky.

(Dmitry takes the bottle.)

DMITRY
Thanks.

YURI
Where is Hazzie?

DMITRY
She is in kitchen making food, a lot
of food. I just got her to make me
some tea.

YURI
How is her brain just now?

                    DMITRY
She seemed to know who I was for a
little while, and I started to tell
her what had happened to us. Then
she offered me some tea and asked me
where my mommy was and did she know I
was out?

                    YURI
Is she alright? She is making a lot
of noise in there.

                    DMITRY
She is cooking and baking piles of
food. If we are lucky some of it
will be edible.

                    YURI
I hope so. I am starving...

     (Yuri sits down.)

...Do you think it is alright to
smoke in here?

                    DMITRY
What do you think? She will probably
ask you if your lollipop is tasty.

                    YURI
Even so, my own wife wouldn't let me
smoke in house, and I don't want to
be disrespectful.

                    DMITRY
Open the window and blow smoke
outside...

        *(Yuri opens the window and
        lights a cigarette, blowing
        the smoke out the window.)*

...Yuri, the News is on. Turn it up,
I don't know how this thing works.

        *(Yuri grabs the remote
        control and turns the T.V.
        up. He then returns to the
        window and sits on the ledge.
        On the T.V., the 1 O'clock
        News is starting. We hear a
        narrator.)*

                    NARRATOR
*...You're watching channel 5 news
with Vicki Jabbervich...*

        *(Five single drum sounds are
        heard.)*

                VICKI JABBERVICH
Hello, I'm Vicki Jabbervich with the
one O'clock news. Prime Minister
Kantcoughsky and Olga Usakov were
arrested today in connection with
yesterday's bombing at the Four
Seasons hotel in Moscow. After being
saved by rescue and recovery workers,
the two incriminated themselves

shortly afterwards over a slice of pizza. Anastasia Bedlumvich reports...

> *(On the T.V., Anastasia Bedlumvich stands outside the* Penachy District Jail House. *In the background, other News reporters and cameramen are seen setting up and testing equipment. Several armed guards wait outside the jail.)*

ANASTASIA BEDLUMVICH
In a few moments, Prime Minister Kantcoughsky and Olga Usakov will be escorted into the jail house to answer questions regarding last night's bombing at the Four Seasons hotel. After a major decline in popularity last year due to the Prime Minister's involvement in the misappropriation of tinned soup, this recent turn of events is sure to be the end of his premiership. With only one week left before the vote, it looks like the Prime Minister's political campaign will suffer greatly and even his loyalist supporters won't be able to save him now.

> *(Returns to studio.)*

VICKI JABBERVICH
Anastasia, what do we know about Olga
Usakov's involvement in these
matters?

DMITRY
That is exactly what I want to know.

ANASTASIA BEDLUMVICH
It would seem that Olga Usakov has
been involved in a relationship with
Prime Minister Kantcoughsky for the
past three years, but how much she
knows about the bombing is still
unclear.

VICKI JABBERVICH
You say that Olga Usakov, the widow
of famous cosmonaut Dmitry Usakov,
has been having an affair with Prime
Minister Kantcoughsky. Do you have
any hard evidence to substantiate
that claim?

ANASTASIA BEDLUMVICH
Since this morning's allegations
against the Prime Minister, several
staff members from The Metrasky hotel
have come forward and stated that the
Prime Minister and Mrs. Usakov have
been meeting there every Wednesday
afternoon for the past three years...

          (A commotion starts down the

*street from where Anastasia
Bedlumvich stands. Prime
Minister Kantcoughsky and
Olga Usakov are arriving in a
police van. Dmitry looks on
engrossed. Yuri puts out his
cigarette and sits down to
watch the T.V. with Dmitry.)*

DMITRY

Three years! She used to get her
hair done on a Wednesday afternoon.

*(Back on the T.V., Prime
Minister Kantcoughsky and
Olga Usakov are being
escorted into the building.
Anastasia Bedlumvich pushes
through the crowd of
reporters to ask a question.)*

ANASTASIA BEDLUMVICH

Prime Minister, are you behind the
bombing at the Four Seasons hotel?

*(Kantcoughsky is in handcuffs
and is being motioned inside.
He turns around to face
Anastasia Bedlumvich.)*

P.M. KANTCOUGHSKY

No, I am innocent. I don't know what
all the fuss is about.

                    ANASTASIA BEDLUMVICH
Is it true you ordered a pizza the
night before the bombing to be
delivered outside of the hotel the
following morning at 7am?

                    P.M. KANTCOUGHSKY
What of it, I always walk that way at
7am, I thought I would be hungry...

    *(Kantcoughsky is motioned
    inside and Olga follows. He
    turns around one last time to
    face the crowd and T.V.
    cameras.)*

...Don't forget to vote this
Thursday. Remember, we can make
Russia great again.

                    ANASTASIA BEDLUMVICH
This is Anastasia Bedlumvich with
Channel 5 News.

    *(The Reporting returns to the
    studio.)*

                    VICKI JABBERVICH
In other news. A boy was rescued by
a squirrel when he tried to climb a
tree to retrieve a bag of macadamia
nuts the furry friend had stolen from
him earlier that day...

(Yuri turns the T.V. down.)

              DMITRY
Scumbag. That Kantcoughsky deserves
everything he gets.

              YURI
What about your wife?

              DMITRY
Her too. They are two slugs in a
beer trap that have dived in
together...

    (Dmitry opens the bottle of
    whisky and takes a drink.)

...Plaaagh! What terrible whisky...

    (Dmitry reads the label on
    the bottle.)

...Glengrenfear - The Valley of the
Green Man; that is like swamp
water...

    (Dmitry looks up at Yuri and
    shows him the bottle.)

...Is this all they had at shop?

              YURI
That's gratitude, I get you a malt

whisky at an extra cost to me, and you complain. I couldn't get my brand of cigarettes you know, but you don't hear me complaining - something is better than nothing. It's probably all that Sweet Cicely tea you've been drinking; it's impaired your tastes buds.

   (Hazzie walks through from the kitchen.)

            HAZZIE
How are you two getting on, did you have a good sleep?

             YURI
Yes, it was much needed, thank you.

            HAZZIE
Well, food is on the table when you are ready.

   (Hazzie leaves and goes back to the kitchen. Dmitry and Yuri stand up to follow her.)

             YURI
You think the whisky is bad, your troubles are only just beginning.

Scene fades.

ACT 2. SCENE 12

1.15pm. Dmitry and Yuri are sitting
at the kitchen table. In front of
them are freshly baked bread, baked
salmon, new boiled potatoes and a bowl
of salad. Hazzie is putting some
butter in a dish and singing to
herself.

                    YURI
Dmitry, would you like some bread?

        (Yuri hands Dmitry the bread
        and Dmitry pulls a face.
        Hazzie turns around and puts
        the butter on the table.)

                    DMITRY
Yes, why thank you Yuri.

                    HAZZIE
Yuri, try the salmon, it's really
nice. Got it from a local poacher
6am this morning.

                    YURI
I must say, it does look good...

        (Yuri takes some salmon and
        puts it on his plate.)

...Hazzie, you said my name. Do you

know who I am.

                    HAZZIE
Well of course I do. You will have
to forgive me for earlier, I forgot
to take my tablets this morning, they
help me out a lot with my brain.

                    YURI
That's alright, I am glad you are
feeling better...

     (Yuri tries the salmon.)

...Hazzie, the salmon is excellent,
very tasty - and that dill and chilli
topping really gives it a zing.
Dmitry, the food is good, try some.

     *(Dmitry takes a bit of
     everything twice and starts
     to eat. Hazzie sits down at
     the table and starts to eat
     also.)*

                    YURI
Hazzie, I was curious about the
barrage balloons in the garden. What
are they for?

                    HAZZIE
Oh, those old things. That's to stop
the planes flying over and spraying
all those biological toxins and

infectious agents...

> *(Hazzie eats a piece of
> boiled potato.)*

...You've only got to look at my back
garden to see what they've done.

> *(Hazzie eats some salmon and
> then smiles at Yuri.)*

                    YURI
You are joking?

                    HAZZIE
Sure I am; had you going though
didn't I. No, those old balloons
were advertising tools to promote
Yakov's old bicycle shop. We brought
them home here when the store
closed...

> *(Hazzie takes a piece of
> bread.)*

...Still, you've got to be vigilant
of those chemtrails. That stuff can
peel your face right off and give you
the worst urinary infection...

> *(Hazzie eats a slice of
> cucumber.)*

...That reminds me. Dmitry, do you
remember your cousin Jess?

                    DMITRY
Who could forget her, big, stout
woman with a weak bladder. Always
complaining about how large she was,
while she ate a whole turkey in front
of you.

                    HAZZIE
That's her. Do you remember her
accordion playing?

                    DMITRY
Yes, that was funny. The only person
I have ever known who could play the
accordion with her feet...

     (Dmitry eats some bread.)

...Not an easy thing to achieve, but
when you are that large, what else
can you do?

                    YURI
I wish I had taken the time to learn
an instrument...

     (Yuri takes some more
     salmon.)

...Can you play anything Hazzie?

                    HAZZIE
Good lord no, fingers like a farmer
and a voice like a frog; but you'll

get to hear some music this afternoon
when the town's folk get here.

*(Dmitry and Yuri look at
Hazzie.)*

YURI
Town's folk, why are they coming
here?

HAZZIE
Well, they always come here after the
Mooncalf Carnival to celebrate
Founders Day. You didn't think I'd
cooked all this food for you two did
you?

DMITRY
Well, I did not want to say anything.
You have been acting a bit strange
since we have been here.

HAZZIE
I know I have, but I'm alright now.
As long as I remember to take my
tablets.

(Yuri puts his fork down.)

YURI
Hazzie, your last name isn't
Pyritevich by any chance?

                    HAZZIE
Yes, of course, didn't Dmitry tell
you?

                    YURI
No, he didn't...

        (Yuri looks at Dmitry.)

...Dmitry, we've got to get out of
here. Half of the town are coming
here to look for some lost gold...

        (Yuri looks at Hazzie.)

...Hazzie, what time do they get
here?

                    HAZZIE
About another ten or twenty minutes,
but that's alright most of them stay
in the field out back with their
metal detectors, you'll be safe here.

                    DMITRY
What is the Mooncalf Carnival and
Founders Day? I don't remember
anything about it when I was boy.

                    HAZZIE
It has always been, but it was a much
smaller affair years ago when you
were a boy. Back then, it was just a
man and his dog jumping through hoops

and one food stand selling raw parsnips. It's grown quite a lot over the years and went crazy after my poor Yakov died. It's my fault really. If I hadn't gone to the bank that day, it would all be different. The town's folk have all got gold fever, they've had it for the last fifteen years. You see, in Yakov's will there was mention of a safety deposit box at the local bank, so I went along to look at it. Inside the box, there was a map that belonged to the town's founder Yagor Pyritevich. The map was full of strange riddles and spoke of a Spanish Captain's gold doubloons buried in Vlogomvich. The whole thing made no sense to me, so after a couple of months, I published it in the local paper to see if anybody could understand it. Well, since then, the town have gone a bit crazy if you ask me. It went from the odd person in the back field poking about a bit with a metal detector to becoming part of the carnival's activities. Now every year when we have the Mooncalf Carnival and Founders Day the town traipse up here and look for the Captain's gold. Hundreds of them, and they all want feeding.

(Outside, singing and loud voices can be heard.)

DMITRY

Looks like we are too late. We will
go upstairs in the bedroom. C'mon
Yuri...

> (Dmitry gets from his seat,
> he grabs some food from the
> table, then turns to Hazzie.)

...Hazzie, don't tell anyone we are
here.

> (Yuri and Dmitry leave the
> table and go upstairs.
> Outside the noise is getting
> louder. Yuri looks out of
> the bedroom window to see the
> crowds.)

YURI

Dmitry, look! There are hundreds of
them, it's like a kaleidoscope of
butterflies dancing along the
track...

> (Dmitry peers out the window
> with Yuri.)

...I don't think I have seen that
many metal detectors before. It
looks like they mean business. What
do you think we should do?

DMITRY

We will get our stuff together and

wait for 30 minutes. At that time they should all be here and the track will be clear. We will put on our masks and slip through the crowd unnoticed, walk to the motorbike and leave. When we get to town, I will find a phone and call my friend.

                    YURI
Sounds like a solid plan. I am feeling better after that food, and I am ready to sort this mess out and get back our lives.

Scene fades.

                 End of Part I

            FIND OUT WHAT HAPPENS NEXT IN:

DOWNFALL - PART II

If you enjoyed this book and would like to be notified of my next release, please subscribe to the *News, Events and Much more* section of my website under the 'Contact' heading. If you have time, please rate and leave a review on Amazon to help increase awareness of this series. Many Thanks, Sam Lucas.

To see the complete collection of books in this series, please go to: **www.samlucasbooks.com**

www.ingramcontent.com/pod-product-compliance
Lightning Source LLC
Chambersburg PA
CBHW051502170626
46811CB00002B/593